FLOWER SHIELDS

A Four Horsemen Novel

By

C. A. King

I0611373

Cover Design: Ravenborn Covers

Editor: J.D. Cunegan

Dedication & Acknowledgement

This book is dedicated to my Readers. Without you,
my novels would be nothing more than words on a blank page.

-and-

To the people who have never given up on me, even in the rough times!

Look for other Books by C.A. King including:

The Portal Prophecies:

Book I - A Keeper's Destiny
Book II - A Halloween's Curse
Book III - Frost Bitten
Book IV - Sleeping Sands
Book V - Deadly Perceptions
Book VI - Finding Balance

Tomoiya's Story:

Book I: Escape to Darkness
Book II: Collecting Tears

Surviving the Sins:

Book I: Answering the Call
Book II: Pride
Book III: Lust

When Leaves Fall: A Different Point of View Story

Miracles Not Included

Peach Coloured Daisies

Shot Through The Heart: A Faerie Tale

Twisted Tales of a Dead End Street

Cover Design: Ravenborn Covers

First Printing: August 15, 2017
Second Printing April 22, 2018

ISBN: 978-1-988301-25-9

Kings Toe Publishing
kingstoepublishing@gmail.com
Burlington, Ontario. Canada

Opening Thoughts

Creation. Over the years, there have been hundreds of plausible explanations for how and why man came into being. The problem that has plagued an entire race throughout the ages was and always will be which of these interpretations, if any, held truth.

Humans have always required knowledge. Where did they come from? Why were they put here? This whole species has searched for explanations locked somewhere in the limits of their own minds. Imagination itself held the key to opening the door. Once unlocked, the possibilities were endless. Myths and legends were born and passed down through the ages.

A simple recanting of these stories has, without question, revealed proof of a common thread between them. Few would argue that, at the root of most origin tales, there existed the acknowledgment of the presence of one or more supreme beings - someone or thing credited for having brought about all life on earth. Where these celestial beings, referred to as Gods, came from may never be known. If, however, one knew where to look, one could find evidence of their time here - or perhaps the scars they left behind.

The following was one of those stories - a love story gone wrong.

Prologue

In a place where creativity through art, dance, poetry and music was coveted above all else, a child was born. From the very beginning, Ihenna, was thought of as by far the most beautiful of her kind. In a realm mesmerized by refinement, it was of no surprise to anyone that, when she came of age to take a mate, suitors lined up with unimaginable gifts to win her hand and her heart.

It was Nakamire who won in the end. His admiration for Ihenna was unmatched. Of course, when he presented his gift, he had no idea one of his nine brothers was in the line behind him. Zahare never had the opportunity to profess his love, though it wouldn't have mattered if he did. Nothing could compare to Nakamire's creation - a world filled with beauty, born from pure love.

This new world was designed in two levels. One, in the open, where plants and animals roamed free and another below, where his bride-to-be could escape to if she became overwhelmed by her surroundings.

It was the surface Ihenna fell in love with. Enough so that she decided to make it her home. A grand castle was built, surrounded by stunning gardens filled with her favourite flowers. It was a temple for his bride-to-be that captured everything she held in high regard. Her future husband had attended to every detail, including the race of man to admire her. They showered her with beautiful words, art and music. Her life was a dream world where only the things she loved most existed.

Being worshiped as a god had a certain, undeniable appeal. Nakamire's siblings and friends quickly joined the proud couple, eager to stay in paradise and share in the abundance of happiness - albeit some relished their newfound roles a little too much. A new race of demigods was born carrying the bloodlines of both the creator and creation.

Unbeknownst to them, not everyone shared in their bliss. Every day Zahare witnessed their love, he grew more bitter, eventually taking up residence alone below the surface world. Blatant attempts to fill the growing void inside him with numerous women failed. A race of half-breeds born from jealousy and rage were his only reward.

Zahare despised this new world. His own offspring became his personal demons - twisting his consciousness further into the depths of insanity. It was there, in the lunacy of his own mind, that a plan took life. He would kill Nakamire and take Ihenna for himself.

Fueled by the words of a madman, his demons embraced the power each inherited - their only goal to be the one to sit by their father's side and win his approval.

When the day came, Zahare approached his brother, deception dancing on his lips in the form of a smile - a poisoned dagger concealed. One prearranged distraction was all he needed to unsheathe his weapon and, with every ounce of anger he had stored, plunge it deep into flesh.

It was over in a flash, but it wasn't Nakamire who lay lifeless on the marble floor. Ihenna used her own body to block the attack. Zahare killed the only woman he had ever loved. Screams of anguish by not one, but two gods rumbled through the skies, quaking the earth.

If Zahare hadn't been consumed by madness before, he was now. Blaming not only his brother, but also the race of man and the world they lived in, he called forth his strongest demons to unleash their powers born from his rage: pestilence; famine; war; and death. Demanding total destruction, he promised to take the most loyal of his spawn to another world - one ruled by darkness.

Nakamire had lost his true love, but he wasn't about to let the world she held so dear suffer the same fate. With half-breeds by his side, a battle like no other ensued. The others, Nakamire's friends and family, once thought of as mighty gods, fled, refusing to be caught in the wake of certain destruction. They were, in fact on the verge of being prophetic.

Heavy casualties were suffered on both sides. In the end, only one could win. Nakamire and the demigods stood victorious, but on that day, there were no feasts or celebrations.

With all he had already lost, Nakamire couldn't bear to destroy his brother as well. Instead, he sealed Zahare and as many of his brother's demon off-spring as could be found beneath the surface world - a jail meant to provide a constant reminder of the atrocities that had been committed. Four locked gates stood between the two plateaus. One demigod was chosen as protector of each gate, should Zahare ever find a way to open them.

In the wake of devastation, Nakamire tried to rebuild - hoping to bask in the memory of Ihenna's happiness. Like so many others, he too turned to female companionship, attempting to fill the void. By the time he realized his mistake, he had already become a father many times over. Unlike the other gods, however, he felt a connection to these demigods. Torn between an inability to remain in mourning and his love for his children, Nakamire was forced to make a choice. With heavy heart he left his creation, allowing only those born of his world to return with him. Zahare, the demons and the demigods were all left behind. That day the gate to the heavens was destroyed, never to open again.

*****

Over time, truths became legends - merely tales passed down from generation to generation. Slowly, the facts mutated - a little sensationalism added at a time until only a thread of authenticity remained.

Demigods and demons alike disappeared. Records of their existence were destroyed. What once was, became little more than the whispers of secret organizations. They, however, weren't gone, but were merely lying in wait, to one day appear again.

The guardians of the four gates remained faithful to their cause through the ages - seeking out and destroying demons trying to free their forefather from the confines of the hell he had been sentenced to live in.

Thousands of years later, a new threat appeared on the horizon...

Chapter One

Morning person or night owl - those are the two categories people usually fell into. That is, except Tara - she didn't fit into either. If anything, she was definitely a middle of the road sort of girl. Her mother often commented she was the *Goldilocks* of real life. Everything needed to be not too hot and not too cold. That translated into not too early and not too late - afternoons.

Flunking out of college had made her change her plans a bit. Of course, her mother and father offered her a secure position working at their funeral parlour. Accepting it would have been the easy thing to do. A love for flowers meant she could handle the sickly sweet aroma - a scent that others couldn't. It was the dead bodies she had issues with.

That meant today, morning was a necessary evil. She needed a job. Armed with a local newspaper and a pen, she boldly set out - determined not to return without one.

The crack of dawn wasn't a particularly good time of day and one Tara hadn't actually seen many of. Cold and damp were the two words that came to mind. There also weren't many people stupid enough to be already out the door at that hour. The early bird can't catch the worm if the worm isn't up yet.

She shoved her hand into her pocket to retrieve its contents: a gum wrapper; a lost button; a few quarters; and a piece of red thread. Her fingers pushed the change around - enough for a small coffee, maybe not at a cafe, but at least at a cheap coffee shop. If she sipped it slowly enough, it might last long enough for the rest of the city to open and the sun to come up.

There was something odd about calling her hometown a city. It was technically under the population requirements to be called one. Yet some big official decided city was what it was. There really weren't many differences between where she stood and the town ten minutes up the road. Perhaps it was the movie cinema on Main Street that made the distinction between the two. It was on her list to submit an application to later, although not her number one choice for an occupation. It wasn't likely anyone woke up to a eureka moment involving a career at the popcorn stand.

Tara smiled. The first thing in a long time to go her way - the coffee shop was empty. Taking a seat at the counter, she dropped the change, letting the clanging sound of the coins alert an elderly waitress of her arrival. They spun around, before coming to settle in a fairly neat pile.

"Big spender, I see," the woman scoffed, a certain amount of sass in her tone. "Did you need a menu?"

"Just a coffee, please," Tara replied.

The woman slid a stained mug on the counter - filling it with a dark liquid. A bowl of creamers and sugar packets fell into place alongside.

"Anything else?" the woman barked.

"No, thank you," Tara answered, looking at the pink name tag pinned to the waitress' uniform, "Maggie." An eyeroll was her reward for politeness.

Not being a morning person also meant she wasn't a big coffee drinker. Three creamers and four sugar packets later and she was ready for her first sip. Her lips puckered up, pressed together. A stream of air passed through on a mission - cool the liquid before it burnt her mouth, or even worse, her tongue.

The outside of the mug rested against her bottom lip. The first drop hit her taste buds. She almost dropped the cup on the spot, gagging. A couple more creamers and sugar packets entered the mix. She didn't need to be a coffee connoisseur to know that batch was burnt. Day-old doughnuts were one thing, but day-old coffee was pushing it. Still she'd spent the rest of her money on it, so she was going to drink it - like it or not. It was that type of determination that she needed today. That was what was going to get her a job.

Re-reading the help wanted section of the paper took a whole ten minutes. She'd already read through the same listings at least a dozen times before in the last twenty-four hours. It was time to accept she wasn't going to find something new she may have missed.

"Maggie," Tara said, "this place wouldn't happen to be hiring, would they?"

"Ha!"

A single laugh was actually a very good answer. The waitress didn't need to say another word.

"I'll take that as a no," Tara said, returning her gaze to her mug of liquid mud.

Maggie sighed. "Take a look around. Business isn't exactly booming. The economy is tough right now. Maybe try back in a few months. Lots of folks are hurting for work right now."

A few months was too long to wait. Yesterday, she'd argued with her mother about working in the family business - maybe even made her mom cry. A swig of coffee washed back guilt.

She pulled out her phone. "Wifi?"

No answer meant no. She sighed, grateful her parents hadn't shut off service. That didn't mean she wanted to run up a bill. Her data for the month had somehow managed to disappear quickly, like every other month.

She typed in *crack of dawn*, still curious why anyone called it that. The answers that came up didn't help much. She was sure it had nothing to do with a girl named Dawn bending over as the sun came up.

"Here," Maggie said. "It's free refill day."

Tara managed a meek "Thank you." She was grateful for the extra drink, but at the same time wondered how pathetic she must have looked to make someone like Maggie feel sorry for her. Normally, she would have refused such a blatant pity offering, but nothing else had opened yet and she needed the place to wait.

A tiny bell rang as the front door opened. Tara glanced over her shoulder at a man wearing an all-black suit walking in. It wasn't so much him that caught her attention, but rather the ring. She was sure it hadn't made any noises when she came in.

"Coffee," the man said, taking a seat in a corner spot at the counter. "Black."

Tara turned her attention back to her mug, forcing back another mouthful. Her taste buds weren't going to thank her anytime soon.

"You bet," Maggie said, a grin painted on her face. "I have a fresh pot right here."

What was left of the coffee in Tara's mouth returned to her cup. Wiping her mouth with a napkin, she hoped a fake cough had been enough to convince her audience she swallowed her drink the wrong way. Not that it did anything to alleviate the weight of the stares in her direction. She didn't have to look up to know she was the centre of attention - it felt like a ten-pound bag of potatoes had been placed on each of her shoulders.

She side-eyed the waitress as she walked by with a new pot of steaming coffee. Closing her eyes, Tara let the fresh aroma fill her senses as it wafted by. It was almost as robust as the scent she adored from her favourite cafe near the college. Those days were long gone.

Tara's eyes opened in time for a glimpse at the man throwing a bill down on the counter. She let out a tiny huff under her breath. Apparently, not all customers were equally important anymore - only the ones who looked as if they could tip well were.

Focusing her attention on the paper again, she tried to forget the other patron. Curiosity always got her in trouble. What was even worse - she couldn't remember anything about his features at all. It was far more obnoxious than having an itch she couldn't scratch.

A well-dressed man, around her age, alone in a coffee shop simply didn't happen in real life. It had the makings of one of the cheesy romances paperbacks she was addicted to written all over it. A wild night of passion and the hero is left searching or even yearning for the woman he can no longer live without.

A chuckle that sounded more like a hiccup escaped her slightly parted lips. "Excuse me," she said, trying to cover up the truth. The red creeping into her cheeks was sure to give her thoughts away. Now she had to know. It would drive her crazy if she didn't at least glimpse. Trying to be smooth, she glanced over in his direction and smiled.

Tara gasped. What was left in her cup toppled over, soaking both her newspaper and part of her white sweater.

"Damn," she groaned, grabbing a handful of napkins from the silver dispenser in front of her. Soaking up the liquid on the counter was her first concern.

"I'll get it," Maggie said, waving a cloth in the air as she rushed over. "Just leave it."

Tara winced at the sight of handfuls of coffee-stained napkins - a waste. Of course, a cloth would have been better. "Sorry," she mumbled, reaching for a few more for her clothes. She sighed. The stain wasn't coming out without a good washing. It wasn't good to show up applying for a job in dirty clothes.

Without resistance, the door flung open, allowing for a quick and relatively painless exit. Tara glanced back over her shoulder. It didn't ring. Again, the door had been the object of her attention - and again her gaze met the stranger's. It hadn't been her imagination. A reflection in his eyes screamed death.

Chapter Two

"I see I'm not the only one to sense something," Michael said, blowing dust off of a thick book.

"Good to see you too, brother," Gabby replied without looking up. She inhaled deeply. The musty scent of parchment had always been one of her favourites. In that room, she had an endless supply. Hundreds of books from every age filled the walls from the very bottom all the way up to the ceiling - four stories high.

"So," Michael said, resting his backside on the library table, "don't keep me in suspense. What did you find?"

A book snapped shut. She took in a deep breath as her fingers ran over the weathered cover. "I thought we'd wait for our other siblings."

Michael sighed. Patience was a virtue the gods had forgotten to give him. It was his belief they used far too much on his sister and simply ran out when they got to him.

"They won't be long," Gabby stated. "They never are." She was the only one of the four who chose to continually occupy their home. Over the centuries, her brothers came and went as they pleased - boredom their constant companion.

"Are we at least sure there is an issue this time?" Michael demanded, flipping through the pages of another book without actually reading a word. It landed on the table with a thud.

"You know as much as I do in that regard," Gabby snapped. "I can only find bits and pieces to help interpret the information we have."

"You'd think after all these centuries we would have a clue by now," Michael said, starting to pace.

"Perhaps if we hadn't been abandoned..."

"Uri!" Gabby cried, jumping to her feet and lunging into a bear hug.

"He always was your favourite," Michael scoffed.

"Jealous?" Uri teased.

"Pull it together. We aren't here to fight each other."

Michael extended his hand. "Raphael," he said. "Good to see you." Their hands slapped together in a firm shake.

"It's Ralph," He commented.

"What's the matter?" Uri asked. "Tired of being named after a turtle? Perhaps you'd like us to order some pizza."

Ralph chuckled. "Very funny," he answered. "Don't tell me you've thrown all this away to become a stand-up comedian."

Uri pointed his fingers and thumb in such a way as to resemble a gun being fired. His tongue pressed against his cheek making a couple of quick clicking noises. "You got me," he said, adding a wink at the end.

"Could we bypass the jokes and get down to it?" Michael asked.

"Honestly, brother," Uri said, throwing his arm around Micheal's shoulder. "We barely see each other anymore. It's been what - two or three hundred years? Sometimes it's good to come home. Why did we stop living here last time?"

"I believe," Gabby answered, "Michael tried to kill you."

"Right," Uri agreed, nodding. "You really should do something about that temper of yours."

"Or, you could stop annoying me," Michael barked back. "Regardless, we aren't here to discuss either of our shortcomings."

"No," Ralph interrupted, "We aren't, but we are going to have to coexist here together for at least the time being."

"You sound like you know something," Gabby said.

A pile of trashy newspapers scattered over the table, covering books containing thousands of years of recorded information.

"Wonderful, tabloids" Michael blurted out. "Light reading for the airhead masses. We aren't stooping that low, are we?"

"Like it or not," Ralph explained, "these are the only types of papers that deal with the signs we are looking for. No one believes in gods and devils anymore. If they do, some doctor tells them they have a mental health issue and prescribes medication to cure it, or worse throws them in an institution and locks the door. The world isn't what it once was."

"It never is," Michael offered. "There is always something in the way of faith. If half the current population knew the truth, there'd be widespread chaos. It's no wonder the gods abandoned us."

"They may yet return." Gabby added. "Perhaps it is us who have lost our faith."

Michael laughed. He picked up a picture frame from the sideboard. He spent a mere second studying it. The picture itself was a sketch from long ago and did little to capture his personality. The other man depicted had been his best-friend, Dante. Only a day later their friendship would end, as would Dante's life. It was a lesson Michael learned the hard way. Getting close to anyone in his line of work simply wasn't possible.

"I'm serious," his sister said. "I don't think they simply left us. There was a plan we were meant to follow. We simply need to figure out what it is."

"I'm glad you are confident," Michael replied, replacing the picture to its proper place. "Excuse me if I don't share in your sentiments. If there was a master plan of some sort, wouldn't it have made sense to let us in on it?"

"We aren't here to argue the politics of our creators," Ralph offered. "Let's make the most of what we can do."

"Okay!" Uri exclaimed. "Where do we start?"

"Simple, we all grab a handful of these papers. If we split up, we can check them out faster and put our minds at ease. Let's hope this is another false call."

Michael grabbed a fistful of tabloids. "I'll handle these," he said. "If the demons are assembling, we better be the ones to find the keys first. I'd rather stop the doors from being opened than have to deal with what is on the other side."

Chapter Three

Even though Tara had soaked her newspaper, she'd managed to remember all of the want ads it listed. When it came down to it, the classifieds would have simply ended up nothing more than a strange form of tic-tac-toe. The O's had already been placed around possible jobs. All that was left was to change them to X's - crossing off each after visiting. Of course, that at least would have given her something to do. Every single position she was applying for had already been filled before she arrived.

It was hard to wrap her mind around the concept of a person being hired before the place hiring opened. That left her without a lot of choice. She'd return home; admit defeat; and end up working in the family business - funerals.

There was one word that came to mind to accompany death - creepy. It was a topic she couldn't discuss. No one ever understood. She had, after all, grown up around it. That didn't make it any easier. In reality, that was more than likely the problem. While her parents always treated the dead with respect, there were others who worked there who had stories - terrifying ones, especially to a young girl. These funeral legends were whispered between ears of employees and, to be honest, had turned her white from fear on many occasions. It was also the reason she loved flowers so much.

Tara was only ten when she first heard about different scents from funeral arrangements warding off evil spirits and demons. Before then, she had assumed, like most others, that bouquets were bought to ease the pain of loved ones. She listened intently to the funeral home lore, including which flowers were most effective. It wasn't a shock to learn lilies, orchids and roses topped the list. Of course, the funeral home myths hadn't done much for her psyche. From that evening on, she was the only girl in her school who wouldn't sleep without a bouquet of death-bed flowers by her side instead of a night light.

After word of that got out, other children shied away from her. Few mothers wanted their children to play with an obviously emotionally distressed girl. If the mental scars from the stories weren't enough to break her, being subjected the ridicule of her classmates finished off the job.

Over the years, employees came and went, but the tales remained a constant. An image of the man from the coffee shop popped into her thoughts. She wasn't sure why.

Death, that's why.

Road lights began to buzz and flicker, preparing for the unavoidable darkness evening would soon bring. She shoved her hands into her pockets looking for resolve, but coming up empty. Her feet simply didn't want to head in the direction of her parents' house to admit defeat. She focused on the noise her shoes made hitting the pavement.

A drop of rain hit her forehead. At first, she had thought a bird overhead might have used her as a personal toilet. Of course, to some, that would be considered lucky. Luck was something she had never experienced - unless one counted the bad variety. One drop became ten, then came the downpour. The sounds of her steps morphed into sloshes. There was something else there are well - first, an echo; then a shadow out of the corner of her eye. Someone was following her.

Tara surveyed her choices. The street was abandoned. Most of the stores in the area were already closed - probably because of reports of the storm rolling in. She jumped, frightened by a crack of lightning crashing down somewhere a few blocks away. Her pace quickened. If someone was still following her, she couldn't hear them over the sound of her own heart beat - pounding promises of a good headache in the near future.

A glance over her shoulder was all it took. Her feet tangled, sending her tumbling to the ground.

"Are you okay?" an elderly lady asked, holding an umbrella over as much of both of them as possible.

Tara was pretty sure she was already as soaked as a person could be. At that point, the umbrella wasn't doing her any good. "I'm okay," she replied, regaining her composure and stance at the same time. "The lightening frightened me." She glanced over a shoulder, finding no one.

"Come in and dry off," the woman offered.

Tara had been so concerned with being followed, she hadn't noticed where she fell. The door to her favourite shop opened, letting a few floral scents escape. It was like walking into paradise, especially considering the weather outside. The storm had no intentions of letting up anytime soon. This wasn't one of those five-minute downpours. It was sticking around for the long haul.

"Sorry, Mrs. Filmore," Tara said. "I didn't realize it was you in the dark."

"That's perfectly fine, my dear," she replied. "I'll put on the kettle for a spot of tea, once we are upstairs."

The Filmore flower shop was the only one her parents recommended from the funeral parlour. When Mr. Filmore passed away a few years back, Tara's parents had footed the bill for the services. After that, many a trip had been made to the family-run store over the years to pick up one bouquet or another. She didn't understand their generosity to a business associate at the time, but after a while, found a certain amount of pride in their efforts in the community.

"Here we are," the shop owner said, "nice and warm. You must tell me, however, what on earth are you doing out and about in this storm?"

Tara's shoulders lifted up and down. "Job hunting," she said. "The weather channel didn't mention a storm before I left." She held her phone up. "Ran out of battery a couple of hours ago." She coughed, trying to cover up rumblings of hunger coming from her stomach.

"Cookies?" Mrs. Filmore asked. "Tea simply isn't the same without a few sweet biscuits to dunk."

Tara smiled and nodded. She was positive the woman had heard her body crying for nourishment, but was relieved she pretended not to. She had experienced as much charity as she could handle earlier in the day from Maggie.

"How odd!" Mrs. Filmore exclaimed, moving lace curtains to the side to peek out at the storm. "There's a man standing across the street and without an umbrella at that. Why would anyone do that?"

Tara sprung to her feet - the curiosity of a dozen or more cats fueling her need to look. She gasped. "I've seen that man!" she blurted out. "He came in the coffee shop I was at early this morning. I wonder what he is doing here."

"You, my dear," Mrs. Filmore said, "may have yourself a stalker." The curtains fell shut.

Tara didn't move. *A stalker - why would someone want to stalk her? Famous people are usually targets - not ordinary girls who can't even find a job.* Startled, she jumped backwards, a squeak barely escaping her lips. Her mind morphed the cheesy romance it had created earlier into a horror film complete with gore and lots of blood.

"It's okay," Mrs. Filmore whispered. "It was only the door locking. You best stay here tonight. I simply couldn't stand the thought of a pervert attacking you if you didn't."

"Pervert?!" Tara cried. She hadn't even considered that this man's motivation could have been sexual. Those attacks were usually reserved for the big cities and not her home. Remembering the man's expression when she left the coffee shop, she questioned that line of thought.

"Relax, dear," Mrs. Filmore said. "Those types rarely have the balls to break into a building - especially not one like this. I have security, you know... and this. Meet Gus."

Tara gasped. As Mrs. Filmore turned from her china cabinet drawer, she exposed a rather large handgun. "Gus," she mumbled, nodding. It was lucky Tara had moved back to her tea; otherwise, when her legs gave out, she would have landed on the floor instead of on a chair. It wasn't so much the sight of the gun that had unnerved her, but rather the sight of Mrs. Filmore waving it around as if it were a normal occurrence.

This lady was, by all normal standards, visually the perfect sweet old lady one would love to have for a grandmother. Her hair was short and grey - not a silver grey, but more of a blue shade. There was no doubt she relished in attending the salon at least once a week to add a few curls. A white frilly apron covered a floral print dress that clung to curves that once might have been very attractive, but now drooped from the effects of the passing of time and gravity. She baked cookies and drank tea and most definitely wasn't supposed to keep a gun in with her finest floral pattern china plates. Silver cutlery maybe, but not a weapon that is primarily used to kill things.

"I know what you are thinking," Mrs. Filmore said. "I admit I was a bit nervous when I first got one." She sat down on the opposite side of the table, laying Gus beside her tea. After a few pats of admiration, she continued, "After Mr. Filmore passed, I was all alone and frightened. I considered a watch dog, but at my age it wouldn't be fair to the animal. A dog of any size would have been too much for me to properly care for. A small dog is useless for protection. That's when I decided to take a few lessons."

"Lessons?" Tara asked over the lip of the tea cup.

"Yes," Mrs. Filmore answered. "I tried all sorts. Of course, I'm no spring chicken. People will tell you self-defence can be done by anyone - any size - any age. That's horse pucky. I simply don't have the strength to throw someone over my shoulder. When my arthritis flares up, I'm in even worse shape. So, what's an old woman to do?"

Not buy a gun, Tara thought.

"I took the bus to the firing range and signed up for a few lessons - that's what I did. After trying a few different handhelds, I found Gus. We've been together ever since. You know, you may want to think about getting yourself some protection."

"I would," Tara lied. "But I can't afford it right now. Still looking for a job, remember?"

"I almost forgot!" Mrs. Filmore exclaimed. "I was just about to place an ad this week. I need someone to run the shop afternoons and evenings. Isn't that a wonderful coincidence?"

"My mother always said there are no coincidences in life," Tara replied.

"Of course she would say that," Mrs. Filmore muttered, barely loud enough to be heard.

"Sorry?"

"Oh nothing, dear," Mrs. Filmore snapped back, a smile returning to its rightful place. "We elderly sometimes get lost in our own thoughts. So, what do you say? Will you come work for me?"

Tara nodded. "That would be great." A job was, after all, what she had set out to find and she did love flowers. Her intuition stayed silent. "When can I start?"

"Tomorrow too soon?"

"Not at all," Tara answered.

"Excellent!" Mrs. Filmore exclaimed, smacking her hands together. "I'll make up the spare room for you this evening. You can head home in the morning, when I'm sure you'll be safe. Now that you are my employee, it's my duty to make sure you are taken care of."

Chapter Four

Michael slammed the newspaper down on the leather seat beside him. As much as he enjoyed driving from one place to another, following leads from tabloid papers had the opposite effect on his demeanor. This latest town had been another wild goose chase.

He side-eyed the paper headline, *Aliens Stole My Cows,* and shook his head. There were no aliens involved - only a drunk farmhand who didn't remember opening the gate and letting them out. No doubt some other ranch took advantage of the opportunity.

He rubbed his fingers over his eyes, allowing them to fall down around his jawline. After a satisfying yawn, he set his sights on a truck stop style cafe. If he was to continue on this farce of an investigation, he needed coffee - preferably black and strong.

The door to his black 1969 Pontiac GTO slammed closed. A couple presses of his thumb on a button and his baby beeped twice - signalling she was safe. Not that his car was ever in danger in the first place. Michael had the look of trouble to him that kept even a seasoned criminal from crossing his path. That car, however, was the last thing he was going to take chances with.

After hundreds of years of watching people he met age and pass on, he finally realized a machine he could keep as his trusted companion for much longer. All he needed to do was replace a few parts along the way. He had already redesigned the inside, including the installation of his personally designed security system and swapped out a few body parts. The engine, however, was one hundred percent original. The way it hummed was music to his ears - the only music he needed or wanted on the road.

A bell rang on the coffee shop door letting the staff know there was a new customer. Michael slipped into an unoccupied booth. To him, privacy was to be cherished and respected.

"Menu?" a blonde haired waitress asked.

"Coffee," Michael answered, looking away - the wad of gum rotating in the woman's mouth making him nauseous. "Black."

A white mug slid in front of him filled with the dark liquid. He had wanted it strong and it was. He watched the liquid swirl around in circles - black like the depths of a demon's eyes. A real demon hadn't been found in over a century. Something told him that was about to change and it wouldn't be reported in some sleazy tabloid newspaper either. As much as he respected his older brother, Ralph had them barking up the wrong tree this time. If they weren't careful, one of the keys would slip between their fingers while they investigated cows.

He lifted the mug to his lips, pausing long enough to allow the burnt nutty aroma fill his senses. The first sip was always the worst. He forced it down, concentrating on the heat rather than flavour. While his taste buds were still in shock, he gulped back a second mouthful.

He surveyed the room. There wasn't much different about this coffee shop compared to the hundreds of dives he had visited over the years. A few patrons who looked as if they didn't have a place to stay for the night took up booths in front of him. The only other customer was a man trying to convince the waitress to go home with him after her shift. Michael had seen that before. The man would fail and come back to try again tomorrow.

He rubbed his temples. The television hanging on the wall in front of him was playing flashback music videos from the 80's. Having to live through that era had been enough of a challenge without reminders.

"Could we put on the news?" Michael yelled out.

The waitress' gum smacked with disapproval. Michael was cutting into her tip-making time from a man willing to pay for attention. Making the most of the situation, she wiggled her bottom as she strolled to the television. "I'll be right back, honey," she cooed. "Don't forget what you were saying."

The news wasn't something Michael enjoyed watching so much as he felt the need to watch. After all, it wouldn't make a difference if he saved the planet from the wrath of hell if the people on it blew themselves up on their own. He hadn't quite figured out how he would stop a World War, but was sure they would come up with a plan when the time came.

"Refill?" the waitress asked.

Michael swigged back the final mouthful. "Yes, please," he answered, extending his mug. He planned to take full advantage of the offer. Who knew when, or if, another would come.

He chuckled watching the sway of her hips as she strutted away. He took a sip. This batch wasn't quite as burnt. Leaning back on the seat, he settled in to watch the news. It had taken him years to perfect, but now, he could block out unwanted noises and focus only on what was important and what the anchorwoman was saying was definitely important.

This is the first murder of the year for our county. Maggie, a waitress in a local coffee shop, was found out back by co-workers in what can only be described as a cult type ritual. No one has claimed responsibility for the gruesome act. We'll keep you updated as information becomes available.

"Excuse me," Michael called out. "Could you tell me where that happened?"

"Sure can, sugar," the waitress replied. "Too close to here for comfort. A couple of towns down, heading south. I hope they catch the sicko soon. I'm frightened to work alone."

"I'll keep ya safe, babe," the man beside her offered.

"You got a good man there," Michael said, throwing a few bills on the table. "Have a good night." He winked on the way out, chuckling at the man's reaction to the waitress swooning.

That was enough fun for one night. If the reports were true, there possibly was an actual demon attack nearby. Either that, or a group of supporters trying to make it look that way. Whichever was true, he planned to eliminate the problem.

Chapter Five

A brisk walk was exactly what Tara needed to unwind. What started as a simple day of job searching turned sour quickly. The one redeeming factor was she had at least found a job, and one she would actually enjoy. She was thrilled with the prospect of surrounding herself with flowers on a daily basis. It might not be the career choice she hoped for, but it was something she'd be good at.

Where Mrs. Filmore's shop differed from other flower stores was she liked to keep a number of bouquets out in the open, for viewing and sniffing pleasure. Of course, that meant a strong floral scent greeted every individual who opened the front door. To some, that was problematic. Tara read, while researching one of her college papers, that between ten and thirty percent of the world was affected by pollen allergies. Luckily, she wasn't one of them. That was probably why she got this job - her nose could handle what others only dreamed of doing.

She chuckled at the realization that the only mark she might make in this world was for having a super snout. That was fine by her - for now. Thoughts of the future made her cringe.

As much as she loved the scents and vibrant colours of different blossoms, they were technically also her undoing. Even setting aside the humiliation from her childhood, there were other incidents. She had, after all, been kicked out, or rather laughed out, of college for writing a paper on the effect of flowers on the spirit world. To her it was science - to her professors it was gibberish. Her lips curled downwards, forming a rather pathetic pout. No one ever believed her - about anything. Sometimes it felt as if she didn't belong in this world. When she was younger she had imagined she was actually an alien and her parents merely found her and raised her. They, of course, never told her the truth. Her imagination seemed to get her in as much trouble as flowers did.

It was like a ray of sunshine found her face on a rainy day when the door opened. Fresh scents of clusters of buds mingled with each other as if performing a mating call.

"Ah," she cooed.

"Better than fresh-baked cookies?" Mrs. Filmore asked.

"Much," Tara answered, the corners of her lips turned upwards like a lovesick school girl. "What would you like me to do?"

"I'm getting older," Mrs. Filmore answered. "I can't do as much as I used to. I would like to spend half the time I normally do in the shop... give the bones a chance to rest. Of course, I'll be upstairs if you need me - just a holler away."

"But..."

"The price list is right here," Mrs. Filmore continued, "and other than that, you'll be making displays every other day. Move the older ones to the back room and toss those past their prime in the compost. We at Filmore's recycle life - no wasting of a single petal. Any questions?"

"Well, actually..."

"Good!" Mrs. Filmore exclaimed. "I am giving you free creative reign. I know you are experienced with funeral arrangements and, as a young woman, I'm sure you have received your share of tokens of affection."

Tara's face turned a similar shade as the bouquet of red roses the shop keeper was putting together. "Actually, I haven't had any successful romances," she admitted. "I guess I attract the wrong sorts."

"Or," Mrs. Filmore said, carefully adding sprigs of baby's breath to the order, "the right one hasn't come along yet. Everything..."

"Everything happens for a reason," Tara said. "Mom always says that too. I'm just not sure how much I believe in destiny being preset."

"Don't think of it so much as preset, as something wonderful being set aside for each of us - something that was always meant to be. We have the choice to accept or refuse," Mrs. Filmore said, placing the floral arrangements in two boxes. "It's like these boxes. One customer chose to leave it plain... another wanted ribbon added. Either way is fine. The contents are the same. The customers will pick them up and give them as a token of admiration, but I think the ribbon adds a little more to the presentation. It's that much more special. Do you understand?"

A blank stare was answer enough.

"Oh, dear," Mrs. Filmore said. "Let me try again. We have choices, including to follow the route made just for each of us. You may be satisfied with the choices you have made, but the road with the ribbon remains that much more special. That path will always be one of your choices, no matter how many times you drift the other way. Life, believe it or not, wants us to find its meaning."

"So you're saying I've made poor choices?" Tara asked. "You really are sounding like my mother."

"No, of course not," Mrs. Filmore answered, smiling. "I'm saying there is a perfect place for everyone - a path that is always there and always will be there. It leads to the box with the ribbon. That doesn't mean there is anything wrong with the flowers in the other box should you chose them."

Tara nodded. She wasn't fully sure whether she understood the premise behind the ribbon psychology or not, but was satisfied the explanation was as full as it could be without becoming painful.

"I'm feeling a bit tired," Mrs. Filmore stated. "I know you haven't had proper training, but I'm confident you can handle it. Would you mind if I took a bit of a lay-down?"

"Of course not," Tara answered. "I'll manage." How hard could it be? The prices were, after all, listed with and without taxes.

*****

A middle-aged man was her first customer of the day. His piercing blue eyes were unlike anything she had ever seen before. He was a bit older - his years exhibited in gentle wrinkle lines around his eyes and the corners of his mouth. Age, however, didn't make a difference in his overall appearance. Everything about him was appealing, right down to the perfect amount of grey running through his black hair. His purchase - a perfect dozen long-stemmed red roses. He added one extra to the order at the end. She almost fainted on the spot when he gave the single rose to her for her helpfulness.

She sighed, watching him exit the building. Someone out there was very lucky. That man was the epitome of a perfect gentleman and exactly the type of man she needed. There was no way she was going to fall for another bad-boy type and have her heart crushed again.

She winced at the thought of her previous romantic encounters - if one could call them that. She fell hard and fast and not once had any of them ever returned the same admiration. Most of them thought she was a bit of a flake by the end of a couple of dates. Her mother always comforted her, saying she was in love with love and one day her knight in shining armour would appear. Tara spent the better part of years hoping for that day before swearing off the type she always ended up with.

The rest of the afternoon flew by faster than Tara anticipated. All of the day's orders were picked up without incident, including a couple of phone requests she prepared by herself.

Her fingers tapped on the counter top. Maybe it was time to wake Mrs. Filmore to go through closing procedures. There had to be more to it than simply locking the deadbolt. It was hard to understand why the shop owner hadn't already returned. It was, after all, her first day.

The door bells rang.

"Hello," Tara called out, carrying a large vase of lilies that weren't quite as perky as the others. They were headed for the back room and eventually the compost.

From death comes life - a neverending cycle.

No one answered.

"Hello!" Tara yelled again.

No one answered.

Tara sighed. The whole scenario could have been the plot for a bad horror movie and her imagination was happy to fill in details. She walked to the front of the shop, peeking around the flower-filled vase still in her hands.

"Hello," she repeated again. This time, the word was directed at someone - a woman, to be precise - standing by the still slightly ajar door.

She was dressed well, in designer clothes. Even from the rear, Tara recognized the label from the outfits most of the popular girls at the college wore. What she couldn't figure out was why the woman wasn't acknowledging her. She inched closer.

"Can I help you?" Tara asked.

"I'm looking for the key!" the woman exclaimed, articulating each word as if English was a second language.

"I'm sorry," Tara replied. "I'm not sure what you mean. Is that a type of flower?"

"The key!" the strange woman yelled. "I'm here for the key."

"Perhaps if you showed me..." Tara started.

The vase hit the floor, smashing into hundreds of pieces mixed in with the lilies. It was all that stood between her and those eyes. Tara had seen them before - in the coffee shop, but belonging to a different person.

"Are you alright?" Mrs. Filmore yelled from the stairs.

Tara opened her mouth, but no words formed. Until that very moment she hadn't known what fear was.

"Move back," Mrs. Filmore demanded, Gus firmly planted in her hand.

The woman took one step forward then froze. She looked down at the mess of broken glass mixed in with petals and broken stems that laid between them and let out a shrill scream.

Tara covered her ears. It wasn't a noise she had heard before, nor did she care to ever hear it again. She watched more flowers fall down to the ground in slow motion: roses; orchids; and lilies.

"You best leave here!" Mrs. Filmore demanded, pointing Gus in the woman's direction with one hand and dropping more flowers from the other.

The stranger crinkled her nose and made a snarling noise before darting out the door.

Tara heard the click of the deadbolt, but still couldn't move. Whatever she just witnessed, it wasn't normal.

"Come," Mrs. Filmore said, taking her arm. "We'll have some tea. I need you to tell me everything that happened."

Chapter Six

Tara sat motionless - the events of the past half an hour replaying in her mind.

"Here we are," Mrs. Filmore said. "A spot of tea to warm us up. There's nothing tea can't cure. I truly believe that."

There were some individuals who language seemed to naturally flow from. Mrs. Filmore was one of those people. It was as if she sang each syllable in perfect harmony with the next. Words floated from her lips, finding a home in the ears and minds of anyone close enough to hear them. Tara found the woman delightful to listen to, even if this didn't seem like a delightful situation.

"Cinnamon cookies?" Mrs. Filmore asked. "They are your favourite, after all."

"How did you know that?" Tara asked.

"We had them before."

"No," Tara disagreed. "We had butter cookies yesterday."

"Well yesterday, yes," Mrs. Filmore replied. "But, when you were a young girl, I used to send over a batch for you with every delivery. Didn't your mother tell you?"

"No, she didn't," Tara admitted. "Why would you make all those cookies for me?"

Why did my parents pay for your husband's funeral? What am I missing?

"Our families have been connected for generations. Further back than anyone alive can remember, that's for sure," Mrs. Filmore answered. "We do things for each other. That is simply the way it has always been. You wouldn't want to break tradition, now would you?"

"Is that why you gave me this job?!" Tara demanded. "Did my mother put you up to this?"

"Goodness no," Mrs. Filmore answered. "The answers to those questions will come - I promise. Right now, however, we need to concentrate on what just happened..." She took a sip from the rose pattern tea cup. "Please."

Tara sighed. She wanted the answers to everything all at once, but that wasn't possible. She was back to choices. Both paths contained answers. One box was plain anger. Put simply, she was pissed off she had been kept out of the loop and wanted to know what the odd connection was between their two families. The other box, however, was dressed in a ribbon she knew as fear. There was no doubt that box would be infinitely more satisfying to open.

"There isn't much I can tell you," Tara muttered, before taking a sip of her own tea. It was a calming blend made using lavender and honey. She'd had it before as a child on unusually uneasy evenings. "You were there for most of it."

"Yes," Mrs. Filmore said, holding the delicate cup in both hands in front of her mouth. "In the moments just before you dropped the vase, something must have happened. Did the woman say anything to you?"

"She asked for a key."

"A key?" Mrs. Filmore asked. "Were those her exact words?"

"No," Tara admitted. "She said *the key*." She rolled her eyes at the difference.

Mrs. Filmore nodded. "Anything else?"

"No," Tara answered. "She turned around and I saw her eyes. They were black and cold. It frightened me." A shiver ran down her spine, leaving evidence of its existence in the form of goosebumps.

"Drink your tea, dear."

"I saw those eyes before," Tara said. "The man from the coffee shop - the one in the rain. They were his."

"Are you sure?"

"Positive," Tara answered, "I know it sounds crazy, but..."

"Not crazy at all," Mrs. Filmore interrupted.

"What does it mean?"

"It means," Mrs. Filmore said. "You are going to be my guest for another evening. I'm not sending you home alone with nutters running around. Let's watch the news while we have another cup of tea to relax."

It's the second gruesome murder in as many days in what police are now calling a ritualistic serial killing. The victim, a waitress in a local coffee shop named Maggie, was well known to locals...

"That's the waitress," Tara stuttered, pointing at the picture of a woman that flashed on the television screen. "From the coffee shop - where I first saw the man - the same one in the rain outside here." A hand covered her mouth. "She's dead."

The room began to spin. This was more than she bargained for. People were dead and she was being stalked. She gasped for air.

Muffled noises - darkness.

*****

Tara yawned before opening her eyes, allowing the scent of freshly baked morning glory muffins to fill every crevice of her senses as possible.

"You gave me a good fright last night," Mrs. Filmore said.

Tara shot up into a sitting position, feeling the aches that accompanied sleeping on a couch as she did. "What happened?" she asked.

"You fainted," Mrs Filmore explained. "A good thing it was on the couch as well. I never would have been able to lift you from the floor. I would have been forced to leave you there all night. I daresay you'd be feeling much worse than you do now."

"Sorry," Tara muttered, stretching.

"No need to be sorry," Mrs Filmore stated. "I have a few errands to run about town today. I'll need you to watch the shop for me."

Tara looked down at the crinkled mess barely passing as clothes that clung to her body. Sometime during her slumber there must have been a nightmare, bad enough to cause her to sweat.

"I've taken the liberty to pick out an outfit of mine that should fit you for now. I can stop by your house and pick up a few things while I'm out. I'll be back before dark."

Tara opened her mouth to speak, but found a muffin going in instead of words coming out.

"There's fresh tea in the pot," Mrs. Filmore said, grabbing her brown handbag and a pair of white gloves. "Make extra display pieces today please, I seem to have ordered too many lilies, roses and orchids. I'd like to get rid of them. Have a good day." She waved her gloves in the air over her head and was gone.

Tara stared at her muffin, still chewing the first bite.

Chapter Seven

Locating demon worshipers over the past centuries gave Michael an edge when trying to find out information. They, like most groups, had leaders who were very intelligent and knew how to remain hidden. Of course, on the flip side, there were also a few who weren't playing with a full deck. Those were Michael's favourites - easy to find and ripe for his picking.

Every city had them, and more than the average citizen would ever know about. Occasionally, when Michael was bored, he'd go bust up a few meetings here or there for fun. They were generally the bottom feeders. Their existence was on the radar, but hardly worth investing time into. One might say they were relatively harmless - no actual demons were involved in their activities. Letting them continue simply meant an avenue for information should one of the four be looking for something specific. While they didn't know anything about the gates or keys, they usually knew of the location of newly founded organizations with higher-ups that did.

This city was no different. He hadn't even walked a full block before a husky bearded man handed him a flyer.

He chuckled. "Stupid losers," he mumbled, under his breath. How could anyone hope to run a secret organization while handing out a map and invitation to join?

The advertisement was always the same. All the organizations chose similar names, in this case *The Church of the Fallen.* The body of the message would vary slightly: *Walk in the footsteps of the damned and find your salvation.*

He shook his head. At least it wasn't far - less than a three-block walk. He locked his fingers together, stretching them out in front of his chest. Each knuckle cracked loudly, followed by a similar noise from his neck. It was time to go to work.

*****

The Church of the Fallen was actually located in the basement under a greasy spoon restaurant advertising cheeseburgers for under a dollar. Michael needed a minute to contemplate what atrocities must go into a burger being sold at that price. That joint could be more criminal than the one he was about to raid.

"Hey look!" A girl exclaimed. "Burgers for a buck. I'm starved. Let's get one!"

Michael side-eyed the group of teens as they entered the building. It never failed to amuse him how oblivious people were to danger. The health of a handful of kids wasn't his problem. He vowed to save the world from annihilation, not from themselves.

Garbage littered the steps going down to the main entrance, which consisted of a wooden door - locked. The area didn't smell much better than it looked. Michael fought the urge to take in another whiff. A few raps of his knuckles and a slot opened slightly bigger than a peep hole. He held up the paper invitation.

After a set of three locks clicked, the door creaked open. A cloaked figure moved to the side to allow Michael to pass into a narrow hallway.

The décor was worse than a cheesy haunted house found in every tourist trap across the country. Lack of lighting and tight corridors set the mood for a good scare. Behind him the door creaked closed, extinguishing even more daylight. The locks clicked closed.

"Hey," Michael called out to the doorman.

There was no answer. Michael glanced over his shoulder. No one was there. The man must have used a secret door of some sort. He knew better than to go look for it. That would be a waste of time. This was obviously some sort of elaborate initiation that had to be completed to gain access to whatever sick meeting was taking place.

He took out his phone. Prior to having phone-flashlight technology, a flip-open lighter was the only source of light for situations like this. Somehow there was something a little more satisfying about investigating with fire - even if it wasn't as illuminating.

The corridor seemed to be going nowhere. To most people, the darkness combined with dirt floors and musty basement smell would numb the senses - to Michael, it was an aggravation. His temper was on a short fuse - almost ready to blow. The hallway came to an end, leaving him with a choice of a path to the left or one to the right.

This whole experience was beginning to feel a bit like a carnival side show. The path to the left was completely dark and boring. To the right was a spinning tunnel made entirely out of black and white checkers. A strobe light flashed furiously. For one inflicted with even the slightest bit of vertigo, it wouldn't have been an option. That wasn't a problem for Michael. One of the bonuses of being an original demigod was not having to worry about this world's ailments.

The choice was obvious! The dark path would be much easier and, therefore, most likely led out of the building or to impending doom and possibly a meat grinder for the fine establishment upstairs. The other took a bit of skill to maneuver through - that would play right into the initiation theme.

A decision was made. One foot firmly planted in the rotating tunnel - the other followed suit. He walked forward, ignoring the visual effects, reaching the door on the other end without issue. It was open, awaiting his arrival.

A new room. At least this one had a bit of space to move around. Michael surveyed the situation. A carafe with goblet set was neatly displayed on a stone altar perched at the top of three steps. The red liquid contained within no doubt contained a hallucinogen of some sort. Stone walls were lined with lit torches that cast shadows to maximize the effects of any drugs consumed. There were ten hooded figures and no visible exits other than the one he entered through. If he played along, he'd be drugged and made to see a whole new world. He had no plans of joining that thrill ride.

"Welcome."

"Thanks," Michael scoffed. "So, which one of you is going to spill secrets for me today?" His siblings probably wouldn't have taken such a direct approach. Perhaps they might have even played along for the information, pretending to drink whatever concoction being offered. Michael, however, was not only impulsive but impatient as well. He had acquired plenty of scars over the years to prove it.

Silence.

"No takers?" Michael asked. "Guess I'll spill some blood first." Two throwing knives landed on their mark. "Two down, eight left."

The hoods flew off two men as they attacked from the sides. A glowing sword appeared in Michael's left hand. He sidestepped the attack on the left while plunging his sword into the midsection of the attacker on the right. A swift kick sent the living assailant to the ground. Spinning around, he let two throwing stars free, pinning two more of his enemies to stone. His sword pulled free and sliced the throat of the man behind him.

"Damn!" he yelled. The others had escaped. It was unusual for Michael to let anyone go free. If there was someone in charge, they'd be tipped off about his arrival now.

He grabbed a handful of cloak of one of the pinned demon followers. "Who is behind the murders?" He asked.

The man groaned.

"I'll ask again!" Michael yelled. A dagger sunk into the man's shoulder. "Who is behind the murders?" He twisted the blade to the left then the right.

"Ahh!" he screamed. "I don't know!"

Michael silenced him with in swipe to the throat. "How about you?" he asked, wiping the blood on the second figure's cloak.

"I don't know!" a woman cried.

Michael sighed. He hated it when women got involved in his work. She, however, put herself in this position. He was in too deep to simply let her go with no answers.

"I'll give you another chance," Michael offered. "I need a name or an address." He waved the dagger in the woman's face.

The stream of urine hitting the floor told him she was scared enough to talk. Whatever she said, he knew would be the truth.

"I don't know who the orders came from," The woman stuttered. "They don't tell me that much."

"Let's start with what you do know!" Michael demanded.

"I only know the two deceased were collateral damage. There is something valuable to our saviour. We were tasked to aid in its recovery." Her lips quivered, adding a blubbering sound to the end of her words. "If we were successful, all of our statuses would have been elevated."

"What is being recovered?" He placed the blade on the woman's bare neck.

"I don't know!" she screamed. "I'm not high enough to know that information. None of us were. We were given the task of watching a flower shop."

"What flower shop?!" Michael demanded, allowing the blade to let out a trickle of blood.

"Filmore's!" she screamed. "We were only to watch who came and went, nothing more."

A loud bang sounded. Michael ducked. Using the altar as a shield, he surveyed the room. There was no sign of anyone. Whoever fired the shot must have left in a hurry. He turned back to finish his inquisition.

"Damn," he muttered.

The woman's body slouched forward, although still pinned to the wall. Blood trickled down her face from a single bullet hole. She was dead. What wasn't clear is if the bullet was meant to silence her or an attempt to kill him. Either way, she wasn't about to give him any more answers now. There was no other choice, he'd have to find the flower shop and see what all the fuss was about for himself.

Chapter Eight

Filmore's Flower Shop wasn't much to look at. Another aging building stuck in a time long past. The whole block needed an upgrade, especially being bordered on either side by fancy new buildings. Of course, that was Michael's opinion. He never understood the value of remembering the past by keeping things from other times - that included century homes and shops. Historical societies had their purpose - recording information that helped locate demons.

This store in particular looked as if it had weathered its last storm. It was narrow and tall with a few dozen bricks needing to be replaced. Michael knew the type. Inside the floor level would be set up as a business. A staircase, located somewhere near the back, led to the owner's living quarters. The front doors of these home and business combos were almost always made of heavy wood with three or more old-fashioned deadbolt locks. Michael chuckled. That wouldn't hold a gang of kids out nowadays.

He tapped his fingers on the steering wheel. Sitting in his car watching wasn't doing anything for him - unless one counted making him more frustrated. Whatever the demon groupies were keeping an eye on was inside. He reached over to the glove box and pulled out a wad of bills. How hard could it be to buy a few flowers and ask a question or two? Small talk wasn't his strong suit, but it was better than being bored waiting for answers to fall into his lap.

Glancing at the sky, it appeared there was less than an hour of daylight remaining. One of the things he despised about being a demigod was his inability to wear a watch. Something about his anatomy made them go haywire and break. On the flip side, he knew immediately anyone wearing a watch couldn't be a descendant of either demigods or demons. They were average citizens meant to live in this world. Even one whose blood contained the minutest amount of celestial DNA wouldn't be able to wear one for long - an hour, maybe two. After that, wherever they were, they would start to fidget and in most cases remove the arm piece to their pocket or purse. Most of them had no idea why.

His car door flung open. If he didn't make a move now, he'd be stuck sitting there overnight. Demons preferred to work after the sun came down. No matter where one went, there was always some type of lore being fabricated about them not being able to walk in light or being creatures of the night. That wasn't the case. The truth was, if one looked close enough, one could tell they were different. In Michael's opnion it was in their eyes - a reflection of the dismal emotions they were born from - the blackness people often associate with death. If humans only knew how wrong they were. What they saw in those cesspools was much worse than death could ever be.

A bell on the door rang as he entered. Michael chuckled under his breath. That was another sign of avoiding the benefits of advancing technology. It was hard to understand not embracing a change for the better. Making use of modern-day gadgets and gizmos made his life infinitely easier.

"Hello," Tara called out. She emerged from the backroom carrying a bouquet of flowers in each hand.

"Hi," Michael answered, thrown off by her appearance. Not only was this store living in the past, the clerk was too.

She couldn't have been older than twenty-five. Yet, from the looks of the flower print dress hanging awkwardly on her frame, she should have been vintage. Not only did it appear as if it belonged to the girl's grandmother, it didn't actually fit her. A messy bun finished an ensemble that came from an era without hairbrushes. The worst part was, if she had actually tried, she might not have been that bad-looking.

Tara stood, blinking. Usually a customer said a little more than *hi*. "Can I help you?" she asked, feeling a tension building between them. She took a step back towards the counter. After her last run-in with a stranger, she planned to keep a distance between herself and this one. He didn't look like a gentleman. In fact, he was the opposite. There was no doubt he was good-looking but in a rough and tough sort of way. The worst part was he was exactly the type of guy she didn't want to meet.

He wore a black leather jacket over an off-white, long-sleeved T-shirt with jeans that were maybe a little too tight, leaving little to the imagination. His long black hair and a manly stubble were the type women adored to touch - at least her fingers thought so. She resisted the urge.

"I was looking for something," Michael said. Words usually flowed well for him. Whatever it was causing him to sound like he had the mental aptitude of a frog needed to go. It was annoying.

"Flowers," she replied.

"Pardon?"

"I assume you are looking for some flowers," she said, articulating each word carefully. She tilted her head, anticipating an answer.

"No," Michael blurted out, his impulse taking over his thought process. She was mocking him. "Not flowers, actually. I am looking for a keymaster."

Tara swiveled behind the counter. "The keymaster," she repeated. "And I suppose you are the gatekeeper?"

"Well, yeah," Michael answered, rather surprised she knew who he was. He moved to the counter, excited by prospective answers. Instead he received a bunch of roses over his head - thorns scratched his skin. "Ow!"

"Get out!" Tara screamed, continuing her onslaught with every bunch of blossoms she could reach. "I'm not into roleplaying with creeps. Perverts like you shouldn't be allowed on the street! I don't know what it is about you crazies all coming out lately, but you can go back to wherever you came from."

Michael retreated to the door. "I'm going!" he yelled, trying to duck from another handful of roses splintering all over his shoulders. "You know you're the one who is crazy!" The door slammed shut before he could finish.

Chapter Nine

Michael sat fuming. It took over ten minutes for him to pick all the stems and petals out of his hair and clothing. Thorns stuck in his favourite leather jacket made him even angrier.

He flashed a wicked smile, revealing his thoughts of running back in. He'd grab that girl by the shoulders and shake some sense into her. The odd thing was, women or people in general didn't usually affect him. Sure, she was crazy, but he handled crazy all the time. There was something about her that was different. She consumed his thoughts, to the point of missing the sunset. Luckily, he didn't miss two shady characters crossing the street.

The hairs on the back of his neck standing at attention was enough to tell him he was looking at two demons. They were making a move, but why now? He was under the impression that up until this point they used followers to watch the place. Michael was hoping to extract more information before things escalated to a full-blown fight. He sighed. It was most likely his presence that forced the demons to act.

There was no choice. He swung open his car door again and made his way to the flower shop. He paused at the doorway, wondering which was worse, taking on two demons at once or another barrage of roses aimed at his head. That was the first time he contemplated that the girl might be in on whatever it was that was going on.

That, however, wasn't the case. He grabbed one demon by the scruff of his neck, throwing him into a display of white lilies.

What flower shop displays funeral arrangements?

That momentary pause was long enough for his partner to tackle Michael from the side. The two rolled around on the floor amidst displays crashing left and right. More flowers rained down on them. It was her again. What the hell was she thinking? Why wasn't she running?

Both demons staggered to their feet and were out the door before Michael had a chance to move.

"I must be getting old," he muttered.

"You!" Tara screamed. She reached for the sole remaining bunch of roses and swung them wildly.

"Will you stop doing that!" Michael yelled.

"Why... should... I?" she asked, hitting him with the flowers with each word.

"I don't know," he said, ducking. "Maybe because I just saved your life?" He saw an opening and grabbed her waist, pinning her arms behind her back.

"Ah!" she screamed. "You really are a creepy pervert. Let me go!"

"Listen, lady," Michael demanded. "You need to calm down. Trust me, with the outfit you're wearing no one is having any perverted thoughts. Now, I'm going to let you go." He took a step back, but not in time to miss a full palm slap on the cheek. "Ow!"

"That's for insulting my outfit," Tara cried, turning her back to him.

"You really are crazy, lady," Michael said, chuckling. "That's a great way to thank someone for saving your life."

"My name is Tara."

"Okay, crazy Tara, how about we get out of here before they come back with friends?" Michael grabbed her arm and pulled.

"You want me to leave with you?" she shrieked "I don't even know your name."

"No," Michael huffed, his teeth grinding. "All you know is I'm the guy that saved you. If you want to stay alive, you need to stick like glue to me - understand?"

She nodded. What choice did she have? Between being killed by creepy men or going with a hot pervert, she'd take her chances with the hot one. Her imagination took over, wondering if there would be marshmallow topping involved.

Chapter Ten

Tara wasn't sure she'd made the right decision. The pervert's car, although very nice, was speeding down a dark road of deserted industrial plants. The silence was frightening.

"Can we play some music?" she asked.

"No."

Silence.

The car pulled up to a metal fence. Michael pulled out a white card and scanned it. The gate opened.

"Where are we?" Tara asked. She swiveled around in her seat, trying to see as much as possible. She watched the gate closed behind them, ominously sealing her fate.

"Relax!" Michael said. "We're almost there."

"That's not possible!" Tara exclaimed. "Where did that come from?" Her jaw dropped open. A mansion wasn't there before. She would have noticed a building that size. She wasn't even sure mansion was a big enough word for the structure she was staring at in awe.

The car came to a stop at the bottom of stone steps leading to the front doors. He slammed the door behind him and started up, his long legs managing two steps at a time.

She gasped for air at the top of the stairs. Her legs didn't have the length required to manage skipping steps. If the climb wasn't enough to take her breath away, the décor inside definitely was. "Just my luck a good looking, rich pervert," she muttered. She wiped her brow and followed him into what looked like a library.

"Hello," Tara called out. To her surprise, a woman answered.

"Hello," Gabby said. "Michael, you've brought a guest?"

"Not exactly," Michael grumbled. "She's more of a clue. I saved her from a couple of demons."

"And you brought her here?" Gabby asked.

"Where else was I supposed to take her?" Michael snarled. "She can't go home. That's the first place they'd go looking for her."

"Uh-huh," Gabby said, smiling.

"I'm right here," Tara waved. "I can hear you. I guess now I know your name is Michael. So, can you tell me where I am and what is going on?" A picture of two men on the sideboard caught her attention.

One man she knew was Michael. The other resembled her first customer at the flower shop - only younger.

"Don't touch things," Michael demanded.

Tara crinkled up her face and stuck her tongue out before turning around. She wasn't going to touch anything. She knew better. There was absolutely no way she could afford to pay to replace anything in this place if she broke it.

"I'm Gabby - Michael's sister. Don't worry about him. He's naturally grumpy."

Michael glared at his sister.

"I'm Tara and he's a bit frightening."

"Frightening?!" Michael yelled. "You're the one who beats people up with flowers."

"A girl has to protect herself from creepy guys and perverts!" Tara screamed.

"Michael," Gabby said, laughing. "A pervert? What did he do? Don't leave out anything!"

"I didn't do anything," Michael scoffed.

"He shows up at the flower shop I work in and says he's the gatekeeper and he's looking for the keymaster," Tara explained.

"I am a gatekeeper and I am looking for the keymaster," Michael complained.

Gabby laughed. "This is priceless," she spit out in between chuckles. "Gatekeeper and keymaster."

"I thought he was going to whip out some marshmallow topping," Tara joked. Seeing someone laugh so hard alleviated the tension.

Tears fell down Gabby's cheeks from laughter. She grasped her stomach and gasped for air.

"Am I missing something?" Michael asked.

"Hang on," Gabby said, gaining her composure. She walked over to a far section of the library and back again. "Here. Watch this when you get a chance." She slammed a movie case into her brother's stomach.

"Yeah, great," Michael replied. "Right now, I need to see a piece of identification."

Tara reached for her wallet in her pocket. "What for?" she asked.

Before she could say another word, Michael snatched it from her hand and removed her birth certificate. "Research," he snapped. "No driver's license?"

"Sorry," Tara replied. "Never learned. Can I have my wallet back?"

He tossed the wallet back at her, keeping the certificate. "Don't worry, princess," He scoffed. "I don't need to rob you."

"Who are you?" she asked.

"You wouldn't believe me if I told you," Michael said.

"Try me," Tara demanded.

"We, Michael, myself and our two brothers, Uri and Ralph, are the protectors of the four gates to hell," Gabby explained.

Tara laughed. "Very funny," she said.

No one else laughed.

"You're serious!" Tara exclaimed. "I see. Michael; Gabby, Uri and Ralph." Her lips pursed together and eyebrows arched. She had to be smack dab in the middle of a crazy farm.

Michael sighed. "Michael, Gabrielle, Uriel and Raphael, to be exact, or better known as the Four Horsemen."

Tara bit her bottom lip. "Do you know how many things are wrong with that statement? First off, Gabby is a girl. I don't recall any girls being mentioned in horsemen lore. It wasn't three horsemen and one horsewoman."

"Tell me about it," Gabby answered. "When the stories were first recorded, women didn't have positions in life. They were thought of as incapable in battle. The men back then never could accept me as a demigod. They wrote me off as a beautiful man."

"Right," Tara nodded in disbelief. "And what about the horses? You drive a car."

"Times change," Michael replied. "I'd look rather silly riding a horse around a city. We opted to let the horses have a break and picked up other modes of transportation."

"But you do have horses?" Tara asked.

"Yes," Michael replied. "They are out back in the barn. Anything else?"

"Yeah, one thing," Tara said. "If you are the Four Horsemen, aren't you supposed to bring about the end of the world? Which one would that make you? Pestilence?"

"If you want to believe everything you read," Michael started, "I have a back seat full of tabloids for you." He walked away, waving the birth certificate over his head. "I've had enough for now. I'll be checking out our guest, sis."

"He isn't that bad," Gabby said. "I think he likes you."

Tara's face drained of all colour. Whatever wacky world she'd entered, she wasn't sure she wanted to stay a part of it.

"The records aren't correct. Nakamire - you may know him as God or the creator - left us here to keep the four gates to Hell closed," Gabby explained.

"Wait, God isn't here anymore?"

"No," Gabby answered. "All the Gods left. All of them except the one locked behind the four gates. Can I ask you something? Why flowers?"

"What do you mean?"

"Michael said you hit him with flowers," Gabby said. "Why flowers? Why not a vase or some other hard object?"

"The first run-in at the shop was with a strange woman," Tara answered. "She startled me and I dropped a vase. The flowers seemed to stop her in her tracks."

"Can I show you something?" Gabby asked, leading the way to a back patio and garden.

Tara's eyes lit up like a child on Christmas day. Flowers were everywhere. Their sweet fragrance carried on a light breeze directly under her nose.

"What flowers did you use as weapons?" Gabby asked.

"These ones," Tara answered. "Roses, lilies and orchids."

"No others?"

"No," Tara answered. "Whose garden is this?"

"Ihenna's," Gabby answered. "She was Nakamire's love. She adored this garden and these flowers in particular."

"I can't believe she'd leave it," Tara said, touching the silky petals of an oversized rose.

"She didn't," Gabby explained. "She was killed. It's a long story which I'm afraid you are too tired to hear right now. I'll show you to your room."

The bedroom, like everything else in the mansion, was lavishly decorated. Everything looked like an original antique. That, however, was impossible. All items age. There is no known way to preserve anything from the effects of time.

"I'll leave some clothes that should fit you outside," Gabby said. "You should be comfortable for the night."

Tara was more than comfortable. She fell asleep before the door closed.

Chapter Eleven

Tara grabbed a pillow and hugged it. She swirled her tongue around her mouth, finding only dryness. She sat up and yawed. After wobbling back and forth a bit, she fell back over.

"That's right," she mumbled. "I couldn't go home because demons are looking for me." A pillow covered her face. She had hoped it all might have been a dream.

"Wait a second," she said, throwing the pillow off and sitting up. "If demons are looking for me at my home, won't they find mom and dad?"

The realization of danger surrounding her parents was enough to make her leap out of bed. She grabbed the pile of clothes Gabby had left for her. Even if she wasn't much use in a fight, she'd be a lot more comfortable wearing Gabby's jeans and t-shirt than Mrs. Filmore's floral print dress. She whined at the sight of her hair. Two days without a brush was starting to show.

Tara slid through the long corridor on tip-toes, hoping not to disturb anyone else. She had already convinced herself it was better to go this alone. Trust wasn't something she was willing to give to anyone at the moment. She needed more information. The image of the sketching from the other room popped into her mind.

Who was the man from the flower shop and how was he connected to Michael?

There was no sign of life anywhere. The light shining into the grand entrance told her she had slept well into the afternoon. Her stomach growled, not being used to missing more than one meal in a row.

She'd slept too long. Panic set in. By now, anything could have happened to her family. Whatever she had gotten herself messed up in, they didn't need to be dragged into the danger. She took in a deep breath of air wishing she had agreed to work in the funeral home. If she'd done that in the first place, none of this would be happening.

All that mattered was getting home. There was no one to stop her. She pulled the front door open and walked through muttering to herself about how she was getting back from the industrial lot. That, however, wasn't going to be necessary.

Tara felt as if her mouth might as well be left permanently open, with all the jaw-dropping the past few days had caused. Doing a double-take of the situation, she almost fell over. None of this was possible. She was standing outside a large office building, only a few blocks from her house. Backtracking, she swung the door to the building open and entered. There had to be a logical explanation.

"Can I help you," a security guard asked.

"Was I just in here?" Tara asked.

"No, Ma'am," the guard answered. "You came from outside."

"Sorry. I thought this was the building I was meeting my mother in," she lied. "My mistake."

"Good day," the guard replied, watching her exit the building.

"Well," Tara muttered. "That's something." She was sure the security guard was marking her face as suspicious. Of course, she couldn't blame him. There was no doubt she looked insane and maybe she was. If she made it through the rest of the day, she was definitely booking an appointment with a psychiatrist in the morning.

First things first - she needed to check on her parents. If she wasn't crazy, they were in danger. In a way, being crazy seemed the better option.

Chapter Twelve

"Good evening," Gabby said, offering her brother a cup of coffee. It was one of the few extras she had allowed her brothers to upgrade in their home. Change wasn't something she latched onto the way her brothers had. History was meant to be preserved and remembered. Modern convenience had its place, but not everything needed to be automated. She still enjoyed growing her own food and gardening. "Did you find out anything?"

"Yeah," Michael answered, tossing Tara's identification down on the table. "She's from a solid bloodline. I just don't know which of the Gods was her father."

"I have a theory," Gabby offered. "I just don't know how to test it."

"Why not share?" Michael asked, fidgeting with his phone.

"You know I don't like making a statement until I have the proof to back it up. Almost as much as I hate those gadgets of yours."

"Those gadgets come in useful in the world today," Michael replied. "Sometimes I think you need to spend a little more time in the here and now. Get out a bit. When you do, make sure you take the phone I gave you. It'll come in handy."

"They don't even work properly here," Gabby complained.

"Just because I can't call or use the internet from here doesn't mean I can't do other things," Michael said, smiling. "The internet would make things a bit easier for your research. Almost everything is available online now."

"I prefer the smell and feel of books," Gabby answered.

"So where is our guest?" Michael asked, changing the subject. His sister was as stubborn as he was. Knowing when to stop pressing her buttons was good survival instincts. "She can't still be sleeping. It's almost dark."

"I haven't seen her," Gabby answered. "You could check. I know you want to."

"What does that mean?"

"Admit it," Gabby teased. "You like her."

"It's work," Michael stated. "That's all. I hope that isn't the basis for your theories."

"Except," Gabby said. "You've never brought work home before. You've never brought anyone home before."

Michael groaned. "I'll check on the sleeping beauty. You continue on with your fantasies."

"Theories," Gabby yelled at his back, "not fantasies."

*****

"Gabby!" Michael yelled, rushing back into the library. "She's gone. I've looked all over."

"That confirms my theory," Gabby replied. "The only ones who can use our front door to come and go without assistance are those Nakamire granted permission to and those who carry on his bloodline. Tara must be one of his descendants."

Michael's eyebrows pushed together. "How on earth did you come up with that theory?"

"The gardens," she answered. "It only made sense. The flowers she used to defend herself were the ones Ihenna loved the most. They had an unusual effect on demons - one we've never noticed before."

"They couldn't stand to be near what Ihenna loved. I suppose we can trace demon bloodlines using allergies," Michael joked. "But that doesn't explain where she went."

"That," Gabby said, "I would have thought to be obvious. If you knew demons were coming here and I was alone..."

"She's gone home," Michael said. "Stupid girl."

"Well it's not like you care about her or anything," Gabby offered. "She's just another bit of collateral damage. The demons have probably taken care of her by now. You must be relieved she isn't your problem anymore." She lifted a coffee mug to her lips.

"Damn it!" Michael cursed. "I'll be back." He grabbed his leather jacket off a chair and headed for the door.

"Mm-hm," Gabby teased. "Say hi to Tara for me. Oh and Michael, don't rule out your allergy theory. I think you might be on to something."

Chapter Thirteen

The sun was already down when Michael reached the street. He muttered a few choice swear words under his breath. Tara was reckless, unreliable and annoying. He added stupid to the list. Who in their right mind would rush into an obvious trap completely unprepared? She didn't even have flowers to hit a demon with if they were waiting for her. A sitting duck was safer than she would be.

He jerked forward, slamming on the brakes. It was worse than even he anticipated. Several houses were up in flames. Smoke filled the air, strangling out any remaining pockets of oxygen that could be found. People were running through the streets in housecoats and pajamas. Some were looking for loved ones, other simply looking lost.

A siren sounded behind him - red and white flashing. He pulled over to the side of the road. Emergency services had arrived. Their swirling light show created a beacon of hope to all those injured and confused. The whole area was a mess.

He stepped out of his car and almost ran into an elderly woman with pink curlers in her hair and a housecoat to match.

"My cat," she cried, a blank stare plastered to her face. "I can't find my cat." She grabbed Michael's arm. "Please, you have to help find my cat."

For a moment, he forgot who he was. "Where did you last see it?" He blinked twice.

What am I doing?

A cat was the least of his problems. He took the woman's arm, leading her to an officer. That in itself was more aid than he usually offered mortals of this world. There were more than enough people who were being paid to save cats standing around.

Michael pushed his way through the crowds towards Tara's house. Much of the road was already barricaded off now. He leaped an orange barrier in one swift motion, ducking into some nearby bushes. If Tara was there, she'd be near her own home.

He stayed low. It would have been a mess if someone had seen him. Becoming suspect number one on a most wanted list wasn't a good place to be, even for a demigod. It would take decades of disguises and staying hidden to recover from something like that. When one was in the business of demon hunting, one needed anonymity.

He sighed. Of course Tara's house had to be the one with the largest flames. He should have thought of that sooner. Obviously, the fire started there. The rest of the block was simply cover-up. He felt a shadow brush by him.

Demons.

The hairs on the back of his neck acknowledged their presence, pointing towards a shed in the backyard of the two-story house. Michael followed his instincts. Centuries of life meant he had the chance to learn what others only begin to understand. In everyone there was a sixth sense - one simply had to learn to trust it.

As much as he wanted to find Tara as quickly as possible, caution was still the name of the game. He sidestepped his way between two burning homes.

If they hadn't been on fire, Michael figured they would have been fairly decent places to live. They were by no means mansions, but they displayed an heir of comfort and modern convenience he respected.

The backyard was no different, having twice the space most modern-day houses were allotted. While that was wonderful if a family wanted to barbeque, it wasn't so great for staying invisible. That wasn't the only problem. Given the current state of the area, Michael was only slightly more powerful than a human.

"Damn," Michael cursed under his breath. Most of his abilities stemmed from his senses - each of which was already overwhelmed by his surroundings.

Water streamed down his face from irritated eyes. Thick smoke from the fires limited his sight. To smell anything other than charred remains would require a deep inhale of scorching ashes. Even then, he couldn't be sure he'd succeed in doing anything other than alerting anyone in the area as to his whereabouts from coughing. Of the other three senses left, two were useless - there was nothing to taste except charcoal, and in an open back yard, nothing to touch either. That left sound. Unfortunately, over top of glass shattering from the heat, the crackling of the fires and people yelling, it was hard to differentiate between other noises.

At least he could rely on his sixth sense, and it was urging him to a far corner of the property. A wooden fence to his left burst into flames.

Security fences - what a joke. There is nothing secure about that. For all the advances he had witnessed this world make through the centuries, it amazed him how something like a fence could remain so primitive.

He side stepped the flames and pushed on towards a large tree. As he approached, a scene unfolded before him. Michael froze, staring at the most surreal vision he had ever experience. He rubbed his already red eyes hoping to erase any blur their watering had caused.

It was Tara sitting on a rope swing that hung from the old tree. Ashes sprinkled down from the sky, resembling snowflakes. Tears cascaded down her pure white, emotionless face. Her body was rigid, as if she were a ceramic garden decoration meant to swing back and forth in the wind.

Michael's pulse raced. He wanted nothing more than to run to her side and scoop her into his arms. These feelings were new and unexpected. He'd had women before, but never for more than a one- or two-night romp. By the next day, he'd forgotten their names. Never had he felt such an emotion for a woman as he did for Tara - a woman he barely knew as a person or in flesh. A dull ache grew in his heart from watching her in such pain. He needed to comfort her - to hold her.

The hairs on his neck reminded him why that wasn't possible at the moment. There were too many shadows. Without proper sight he could only rely on his intuition that there were at least six demons in the vicinity. They hadn't reached her yet, but it was only a matter of time. He wasn't about to let them touch a single hair on her head.

He summoned a sword. Even its bright glow didn't cut through the dense smoke that surrounded them. Closing his eyes, he let his instincts take over and lunged to the right, slicing through the midsection of the first demon. He sidestepped an attack, swinging around to land a fatal blow to another, but not before it shrieked a war cry. The others were on the move. He dashed for the tree. Four on one wasn't the type of odds he liked, especially in his surroundings.

"Tara!" he yelled. She didn't answer.

Stupid girl. Why doesn't she run?

Michael stood fast, swiveling his stance from side to side. Anticipation of the first move was crucial. He couldn't see them, but knew they were closing in - surrounding them like a wild pack of dogs stalking prey. He tightened his grip, the sword looking more like a baseball bat in his hands than a sharp blade. He sliced at the air, cutting nothing but smoke. The hair on his neck was standing straight up. The demons were within striking distance. Their lack of attack meant he wasn't the only one whose senses were dulled.

Michael chuckled. He'd survived generations by not caring about those who became collateral damage, how ironic he should be taken out because of feelings for a woman he barely knew. He glanced back at her, squinting to make out her features.

"Hey, you four!" a voice yelled from beside the burning house. "What are you doing?"

Firemen.

One demon let out a cry and the four retreated. Michael turned to Tara still swinging back and forth. He draped his jacket over her shoulders and picked her up in his arms.

"What are you doing here?" the fireman repeated.

"She lives here. I think she's in shock," Michael answered. "There were a handful of other men. I think they might have been looters. You scared them away."

The man looked Tara over and nodded. "Get her out of here. This whole place isn't safe. We're evacuating several blocks until we get the fire under control. Looters are the least of our concern at the moment, but we'll keep an eye out for them. Do you know if there was anyone else inside?"

Michael looked at the house and shook his head. "No, they must have been out."

"Are you sure?" Tara squeaked.

Michael tightened his hold on her. "Yeah," he answered. "I'm sure."

Chapter Fourteen

Tara looked over at Michael. He looked so natural driving that car. It was almost an extension of his own body.

His body. Wow!

It was the first time she'd seen him without his jacket on. She pulled the leather up around her tightly and inhaled his musky scent before looking back again. She wet her lips. He was definitely a fine male specimen by any standards. His long sleeve t-shirt did little to hide his muscular build. Tara bit her lip, holding back the urge to run her hands over his biceps.

She smacked the side of her head. trying to loosen whatever cobwebs that had formed. This wasn't her. She didn't go crazy over bad boys with a few well-placed muscles. His were definitely well-placed.

"Ah!" she blurted out, amazed at how easily she fell back into lusting after the man beside her.

"Are you alright?" Michael asked.

"Yeah, sorry," she muttered. "Everything is a bit overwhelming at the moment. Where are you taking me?"

"Back," he said.

"I need to find my parents," Tara demanded. "I can't leave them. They could be in danger."

"You are in danger and I need you safe," Michael disagreed.

"Why?"

"What do you mean, why?" Michael yelled.

"I mean why?" she responded. "Why do you need me safe? Why should I trust you?"

"What have I done to earn your mistrust, other than saving you twice?"

He had a point, but she needed more. "What about the picture?"

"What picture?" Michael asked, his voice raising with every word.

"The one in your house - of you and the other man. How does he fit into all of this?" Tara asked.

"I don't know what you are talking about," Michael answered, side-eyeing her and watching the road at the same time.

"Of course you don't!" Tara exclaimed. "I want to know what game you are playing. The man in the picture - I saw him. He came into the flower shop the day before you did."

The car came to a squealing stop. "That," Michael said, "is impossible."

"No," Tara disagreed. "It was him. He was a little bit older, but it was definitely him. He came into the shop to buy some roses. He bought an extra one and gave it to me."

"It couldn't have been him," Michael whispered, "because that man is dead."

"Are you sure?" She immediately wished she hadn't asked. There was a sadness in Michael's eyes she hadn't seen before - a deep-rooted emotion. She didn't think it was possible, but that glimmer made him more attractive.

"Yeah," Michael answered. "I'm sure. He was my best friend and I watched him die. There was nothing I could do to save him. That was a long time ago, but I'll never forget."

"I'm sorry," Tara muttered, trembling. She had awoken something in the tough man that had been buried in centuries of oppression. One part of her was glad he had opened up to her - even if it was only a little. Another was furious for disturbing painful emotions.

"It was an age where demigods and demons still battled in the open - a time all but forgotten by this world. A group of us were following a lead we had stumbled upon about a group of demons hiding out in a cave. We spent most of the day climbing a mountain, only to find out the whole thing was a setup. It was a trap. We willingly walked right into an ambush - outnumbered and surrounded. Dante dove right into battle, pushing as many away from the rest of us as possible. I had my hands full with a dozen part demon men of my own. After the last went down, I looked around to see who needed the most help. Dante had a horde on him, but Gabby was on her back facing certain death. I rushed to save her. I never thought Dante would ever fall. He was the strongest fighter I knew - my friend and mentor. I had barely moved a foot in his direction when I saw a blade plunge into his midsection. I can still hear the demon victory cries as Dante staggered backwards and fell from the peak. I ran to the edge, but it was too late. I made every demon and their followers left on that mountain pay for what they did. To this day, I feel no mercy for their kind."

"There was nothing you could do," Tara whispered, wiping away her own tears. "At least you tried. Imagine how you would feel if you had to live with the what if's of not even doing that. Please don't make me live with the possibility I could have done something. It would be worse than any hell I could imagine."

Michael nodded. His gaze fell on her face. A warmth grew between them - and understanding. His hand wiped a stray tear from her cheek.

"Where is the funeral home?" he asked, offering a meek smile. "We have time for a quick stop."

Tara held a hand under her nose and sniffled. "Thank you," she said. "It isn't far. You'll need to take the next right." She paused, watching the houses and buildings pass by. "Can I ask you another question?"

Michael laughed. "Why not, I've told you more in this car ride than I'd admit to my own kin."

"When I left your home..."

"Did you like that?" Michael interrupted. "It's a unique place. Where did you end up?"

"A government building three blocks from my house," Tara admitted. "Is that normal?"

"If you think about where you want to be as you leave, you will end up walking out of the closest deserted building or public building available."

"Anywhere?" Tara asked. "I could have thought of a fantastic foreign destination or a hot island?"

"Yes," Michael answered. "If that is where you wanted to go."

"Anyone can do this?" Tara questioned. "No plane tickets or reservation needed?"

"No," Michael said. "Only those given permission or born of the same bloodline as Nakamire can use the door."

"Was I given permission?" Tara asked.

"No," Michael admitted. "You weren't."

"That means..."

"You must be a direct descendant of Nakamire," Michael said, finishing her sentence.

Silence.

Chapter Fifteen

If the lightning flashing on the horizon was any indication, a bad storm was quickly approaching. Tara counted under her breath. She reached ten when a low rumbling sounded. Two miles away wasn't far enough. Drops of water cascaded down the windshield for a few moments before being swished away.

Tara sat mesmerized by the timed, back-and-forth motion of the black wipers. As soon as it appeared her vision was about to be impaired, the blades cleared the view. It was almost as if the motor could sense the need for its services.

The pitter-patter sound grew steadily. Lightning cracked again. This time she barely had the chance to count to two. The storm was almost on top of them.

The funeral home parking lot contained only one car other than the one they were in - her parents'. The lights, including the street ones, were off. Lightning struck with a loud boom, hitting something, probably a tree, nearby. The front door swung wildly in the wind, visible only in the storm's anger illuminating the sky for split-seconds at a time.

"Wait!" Michael yelled.

It was too late, the passenger side door flung open. Tara ran for the entrance, rain pelting down on her head.

Stupid girl!

His car door slammed behind him. Grumbles of his disapproval were drowned out by thunder. It was less than ten steps to inside, but his clothes dripped, leaving a trail of water behind him. If that wasn't bad enough, every step he took was accompanied by a swish and squeak from his drenched shoes on the marble-like tiles.

So much for the element of surprise.

The entrance way was dismal - decorated in boring grey tones right down to the floors. Of course, there was little more one could expect for a funeral home. While there are a few religions that celebrated a life after a loved one has passed on, they weren't considered the norm.

Mourning... grieving, that's what happens here.

Tara screamed.

Michael's heart pounded as fast as his feet moved. He rushed into an adjoining room.

"Are they..." he started.

"No," Tara blurted out. "They worked here. I don't understand. There are flowers everywhere." She stood over top of the two lifeless bodies, watching blood trickle down their foreheads. They were killed in exactly the same way - a single bullet to the head. If it weren't for that mark, their bodies could have been like any other stiff the funeral home had housed over the years. Both wore black suits over a white full-length dress shirt - their bodies void of any jewelry or colour.

"They've been shot," Michael said. "It's recent, too. Whoever did this is most likely still here. Tara, demons don't carry guns. They don't need them. A human did this."

Tara nodded. Her stomach churned with guilt. There had been no remorse for the two workers when she found them - only relief they weren't her parents. They deserved better, even if she hadn't known them well.

She glanced back over her shoulder as they exited the room. A wave of sadness smacked her across the face, leaving a mark. Perhaps it was the way they fell - their hands outstretched as if trying to touch each other. There was a story they were telling in death - the two had cared enough to try to connect in their final moments. There was no indication of whether in life they had been lovers or siblings, only that they shared a bond. There was love on some level flowing between their already stiffening bodies. She winced, realizing she'd probably never know their story.

Michael's heart wrenched watching her as she fought the stinging sensation in her eyes - holding back tears.

The swoosh of Michael steps grew louder the further in the building they went. It didn't matter how careful he tried to be.

A quick tug on his arm stopped him in his tracks. Tara nodded towards a barely ajar door. A light stood out in the darkness coming from the back office. Her hand trembled in his grip - he knew she was frightened, but not for herself. She was frightened of what she would see - that it would be her family in this room. He did his best to block her view with his body. With two fingers he pushed the door. It flung open.

Tara screamed. Two more bodies lay hunched over a desk. This time she knew them - every feature - every detail. Tears ran freely down her face. A tap that, once turned on, wouldn't be easily shut off. Her shoulder brushed his as she pushed by him, falling to her knees. There was no doubt the two bodies were Tara's parents and she blamed herself.

He knew exactly what she was feeling. The what if's that were racing through her mind. If she had warned them, maybe this wouldn't have happened. If she had been there, maybe she could have stopped it. He also knew it wasn't true. He'd brought her there to alleviate those very feelings, but, in reality, it only made them worse.

"There was nothing you could do," Michael whispered. "You tried. It's more than most people would have done." He knew from experience that wasn't going to console her grief, but it was the best he had to offer. He knelt beside her, taking her hand in his.

"If I had listened," Tara cried. "If I had taken the job here and not become mixed up in all this..."

"Whoever did this would have come no matter what you did," Michael interrupted. "There really was nothing you could do. Your parents must have told you something about your bloodline. It's hard to believe they kept it a secret all this time."

"Nothing," Tara muttered, swallowing back the salty taste of her own tears. "I never knew anything. I'm not even sure I believe all this. I keep thinking I'll wake up and it was all just a really bad dream."

"That's not good. For what it's worth, it isn't a dream," Michael offered. "Whoever is behind this will keep coming until the find what they are looking for."

"A key," Tara whispered.

"Yes," Michael replied. "It is said the direct descendants of Nakamire are tasked with keeping the keys to the four gates of Hell safe. We already know you are a direct descendant."

"I don't know anything about a key!" she yelled.

"I believe you," Michael replied. "Your parents, however, did. That's why they were killed - not because of you. You can't blame yourself. By hiding this all from you, they left you completely unprepared."

"I don't understand any of this. Why do people want a key to unlock Hell?"

Michael sighed. "Only one true God as we know them remains in this realm. That God is locked behind the gates. Some mistakenly believe they will be saved if he is released."

"But if I don't know anything," Tara started, "how can I help?"

"There would have been others who helped your family," Michael explained. "Another family who were in some way connected to yours for generations."

"The Filmores," Tara blurted out.

"The flower shop owners?" Michael questioned.

"Yes," Tara answered. "I never understood the connection of their family to my own. It was strange and even stranger that Mrs. Filmore knew so much about me."

"I think we need to speak to them," Michael stated.

"Mrs. Filmore is the only one left," Tara said. "Her husband passed away a while ago."

"We need to get to Mrs. Filmore before someone else does. Her life might be in danger."

Chapter Sixteen

Lightning lit up the sky with a crack. Those momentary flashes were the only relief from darkness. Even the car headlights were lost in the downpour - rendered useless. The rain showed little signs of stopping. If anything, it was coming down harder than it was before. Pooling water sprayed up from the tires, splashing against the sidewalk. Luckily, no one was out in that weather to be hit by the muddy liquid. The black car pulled up in front of the flower shop.

"Are you okay?" Michael asked. "I can check things out alone if you would prefer to stay here."

The passenger side door opening was the only answer. Tara headed for the door, receiving a further saturation of her clothing.

"Okay then," Michael said, following. "Wait." His face almost touched the glass window. He held one hand over his eyes, trying to see inside. "Someone's been here. The mess from the fight has been cleaned up." He wiped the fog his breath left behind and tried to see more.

Tara stumbled backwards, almost falling. She hadn't expected the door to open when she tugged on it. It should have been locked. She glanced at Michael. He nodded and took the lead. The inside was void of any indications there had been a struggle there at all.

"I don't understand," Tara whispered. "There was a lot of damage. How did it get fixed so fast? Why was the door unlocked?"

"Where would Mrs. Filmore be?" Michael asked.

Tara nodded at a set of stairs. They had only made it up three of them when the wood underneath their feet let out a loud crack. The door at the top swung open.

"I don't know who is down there!" Mrs. Filmore yelled. "I am giving you to the count of three and then I'm letting loose a round of bullets."

"Mrs. Filmore. It's me, Tara. Don't shoot."

"Tara?" Mrs Filmore echoed. "Well, for pity's sake, child, come up. You darn near gave me a heart attack." She plopped into a chair, one hand covering her heart. "You have no idea how glad I am to see you. I thought you were lost or worse."

"Sorry," Tara offered, kneeling by her side. "We wanted to make sure you were okay."

Mrs. Filmore took a few deep breaths. "I'll be fine," she muttered waving her hand at Tara. "You two look like drowned poodles. Stay put. I'll grab you some towels."

"Tara," Michael started.

"Here we are," Mrs. Filmore said, returning. "Dry towels and a couple of robes."

"I'm not sure we have time to undress," Michael said. "There is a lot we need to discuss."

"Don't be silly," Mrs. Filmore complained. "It won't take long for me to throw your things in the dryer. You two change and I'll put on some tea."

"It would be nice to be dry," Tara said, shrugging her shoulders. "I don't have your advanced immune system. I'll be sick as can be if I stay like this."

"Fine," Michael conceded, mumbling a few choice words under his breath. He grabbed a couple of towels and a robe before turning around.

Standing back-to-back, they stripped off their wet clothing. In a moment of weakness, Tara glanced over her shoulder. Her eyes alternated between his finely chiseled physique and an array of scars, presumably from battles fought long ago. She wondered how many there were and if he had a story to go with each.

"If you get to look," Michael said, "I do too."

Tara gasped, her head jolted back in front of her. She pulled on the pink robe that she'd been given. Her clothes neatly piled, waiting for the dryer, she turned around. Her hand covered her mouth, trying to stop laughter from escaping. It failed.

"Go ahead," Michael said, nodding his head. "Get it over with. Laugh it up."

"I'm sorry," Tara said, still chuckling. "You look... gorgeous."

Michael placed his hands on his hips. The position didn't help the onslaught of laughter. He looked down and sighed. The blue and white floral print robe was bad enough, but on his structure, it barely covered his private parts.

"You should show off your legs more often," Tara joked, gasping for air.

Michael piled his clothes on top of hers then took a seat, being careful to keep everything that wasn't meant for roaming eyes hidden. "There are a couple of things that are bothering me. Something isn't adding up. I think I should have kept my clothes on," he admitted.

"What?" Tara asked. "I don't think she is going to try to take advantage of you, if that's what you are suggesting."

Michael shook his head. "It's not that..."

"Here we are," Mrs. Filmore said. "Hot tea is just what you two need to take the chill out of you. Drink it up while I pop these in to dry. Well go on. It's the pick-me-up you need after all you've been through today. I am so sorry about your parents. I don't know what this world is coming to." She disappeared again.

"This is my favourite tea," Tara said. She handed him a cup before pouring one for herself. Her nostrils flared, taking in the aroma. Puckered lips blew on the hot liquid, before allowing it to pass through to her pallet. She closed her eyes, savouring the taste.

"Tara," Michael called out.

"Hm?" she answered. "Isn't it wonderful?" She took another mouthful. "At least try it."

Michael grumbled, but drank the whole cup in one go. "Happy?" he asked.

"Did you even taste it?" Tara complained.

"Tara, something here isn't right," Michael explained. "The door downstairs being unlocked; the mess being gone; this woman didn't even ask what happened or if you were okay."

"You are being paranoid," Tara replied.

"Maybe," Michael said. "But I think we should be careful." He rubbed his eyes. Blinking several times, he shook his head. "What kind of tea is this?"

"It's Tara's favourite," Mrs. Filmore answered, leaning in the door frame her hands crossed over her chest. "Do you like it?" she cackled. "I was worried for a moment you weren't going to drink it. That would have been a mess. I might have had to shoot you." Gus waved wildly around in her hand.

Tara's fingers ran over her lips. There was no feeling. Her movements slowed. "My mother used to give it to me at bedtime," she muttered. "How did you know my parents were dead?"

"Oh," Mrs. Filmore said, moving closer. She placed Gus under Tara's chin, holding it up. "Because I killed them, of course." The gun pulled away.

Michael watched Tara fall to her knees. He tried to reach to her, but could manage little more than to stagger a few steps before falling himself. He closed his eyes, hoping to lock out the spinning room. A cold sweat took over his body. He breathed deeply, fighting the urge to pass out on the floor. How could he have been so stupid? Falling for a woman had made him weak. Her image filled his mind. She was everything to him and he had failed her.

"The tea," Tara whispered. "My mother gave it to me to help me sleep. You drugged us. Why?"

"Yes," Mrs. Filmore answered. "I did. I'm afraid you'll have to wait to find out why. You won't be awake long enough to hear the answer."

Chapter Seventeen

Michael opened one eye at a time. Satisfied the room wasn't going to be whisked away in the middle of a tornado again, he opened both together. Licking his lips proved to be a task worthy of a warrior. Still, he took it on - without success. There was only one way his mouth could have been drier - if he were forced to drink sand. Even tongue wiggling wasn't helping. He pressed his tongue hard against the roof of his mouth, trying to squeeze out whatever saliva was hiding in glands. In the end, a couple good smacking noises was all he could muster.

It was time to move on to bigger problems. His feet rubbed against the cold smooth surface lying beneath them. It was a metal of some sort, no doubt attached to the chair he was sitting in. With every ounce of power, he flexed the muscles in both his arms and pulled up. The restraints around them didn't budge. For the next exercise, he tried moving his legs. The results were even less impressive.

"Damn," Michael muttered. "What's this stuff made of?" Either his demigod strength had been rendered useless, or someone had found a stronger substance to bind him with. The later was more likely. He shook his head. Perhaps Gabby was right - modern day advancements weren't always a good thing.

"It's a new metal."

Michael froze. He knew the voice. "Dante. How?"

"Yes, It's me. Are you surprised?" The sound of chair legs screeching metal on metal accompanied footsteps. Dante tossed a seat in front of Michael. Rounding it, he grabbed the back, threw one leg over and straddled the base before lowing himself into a sitting position. "How have you been, old friend? You've looked better. Although, I have to admit that robe suits you well. The flowers bring out the colour of your eyes. I had to hide you away in here. There were too many men and women distracted from their duties trying to catch a glimpse of what is barely hidden. You always did know how to turn heads."

Michael turned his palms upwards as best he could. "I have been better," he answered, shrugging his shoulders. "It's all the old crow had to offer. I didn't think she could handle me stark naked. What about you? You're looking good for a dead man."

Dante chuckled. "Yes, I suppose I am. You are probably curious what happened. Would you like me to tell you the story?"

Michael smiled. "I've got nothing better to do." He tugged on the restraints. "For the moment."

"When I fell that day, I thought I was dead," Dante explained. His face turned solemn. "For years after, I wished I had been. Then things began to make sense. I saw the world from a new perspective. I'd been missing the bigger picture."

"Sounds like you had it rough," Michael said, still tugging at the restraints. "Was it a self-help seminar? I hear those are brutal."

"Worse. You have no idea what I went through," Dante replied, smiling. "As I was falling, two winged demons snatched me out of the air. I passed out shortly thereafter from my wounds. When I awoke, I was too weak to fight them. They nursed me back to good health. It wasn't pretty, and neither were they. As payment for my debt to them, they required I father their children. That took more courage than any battle I had seen." His brows arched, allowing his eyes to widen. "In that time, I did a lot of thinking. I realized I was fighting on the wrong side."

"Sounds to me like you were delusional rather than thinking straight," Michael snapped. "Or perhaps the companionship was simply too good to give up."

Dante howled a laugh. "Tell me, good friend, how ironic is it that demons saved my lives and not those I trusted to have my back?"

"I tried to save you!" Michael exclaimed.

"Not hard enough!" Dante roared back. "Did you even look for the body? Did you come to save me? No. None of you did. For years, I believed I would be rescued. It was the only thing that kept me going. I believed in you."

"I saw you fall," Michael whispered. "I moved faster that day than ever before. I was still too late. You were my friend... my mentor. I would have done anything to save you. "

"Not anything. You made a choice," Dante replied, shaking a finger in Michael's face. "You chose to save your sister. I understand that. Blood is thicker than friendship. Tell me, though, why did you not look for my body? Did I not deserve a warrior's burial?"

"That's hardly fair," Michael complained, choking on the words. "I had no way to know you were in trouble. Gabby was facing certain death. Afterwards, we continued fighting. With you gone, we almost lost that day. My anger over what happened to you was all that kept me going. By the time the battle was won, days had passed. I went down the side of the mountain, to the river below. I assumed your body had washed away. For weeks I followed the flow, searching. When it emptied into the ocean, I knew there was no chance to find a body. If there had been a shred of evidence you were still alive - any proof at all..."

"Well," Dante said, smiling. "That's all water under the bridge now - so to speak. In time, I grew to appreciate the demon way. I even took the two who saved me as my wives."

"Congratulations," Michael replied. "I'll have to remember to have Gabby send you a wedding gift. Did you register somewhere?"

Dante laughed. "You are still the same. That mouth of yours always did get you into trouble - and me too."

"Why am I here?" Michael asked. "After all this time, why settle a grudge now?"

"You have it wrong," Dante replied. "You aren't the one I wanted to find."

"Tara," Michael muttered, one arm breaking free from the restraints. "What do you want her for?"

Dante held up one hand, motioning for guards to move back. "It's fine. Leave him," he ordered. "You two can go tell the research department their latest product failed. He won't be a problem."

"What makes you so sure?" Michael asked, freeing his second arm. "I don't recall agreeing to play nice."

"Because," Dante answered, "you want the same information we do. We need the girl to find the key. Relax, she doesn't have to die. All we need is a bit of her blood. Don't look at me like that. By now you already know she is a blood relative of Nakamire. Don't play me for a fool. At least give me that much respect."

"Alright. What makes you think you know how to find the key?" Michael asked.

"You would be amazed at what demons and their followers have their hands in," Dante explained, lighting a cigarette. He inhaled deeply then released the smoke into Michael's face. "An archeological dig they funded turned up some ancient scrolls, with some rather interesting rituals. One of which was to unlock the key to the first gate. It was all purely by chance. If I hadn't recognized a few words on the scroll myself, they might not have even realized what it was. Of course, at that point it was still a longshot. A few words in different context could have meant anything. I took a gamble and it paid off."

"What about the other three?" Michael asked.

"We are still working on them," Dante admitted. "I thought I'd give this one a go to see if it actually does anything before wasting too many resources looking for more."

"What makes you think I won't try to stop you?"

Dante laughed. "You want that key as badly as we do - even if it is for different reasons. I know you. You are curious and conceited. No, you won't make a move unless the key is before your snout. Then, you and I may have a problem." He winked, pointing with two fingers, the cigarette lodge between them. "As for the girl, we both know women mean little more to you than an evening of fun. Ah yes, I have kept tabs on you over the years."

"So where is this scroll? I'd like to see it for myself."

"I'm not stupid," Dante replied, shaking his head. "The scroll is almost as good as the key itself. It has taken our research team centuries to decipher it fully."

"The same research team responsible for this?" Michael motioned to the broken metal restraints. "What is this stuff, anyways?"

"A failed experiment, apparently," Dante answered, tossing what was left of his cigarette on the floor and extinguishing it with his shoe. "The best minds in the world are attempting to make an unbreakable metal - even by a God's standards. The floor, chair and cuffs are made of it. I almost thought we had you pinned down."

"Always happy to be a guinea pig." Michael chuckled. "How about you undo the leg clamps?"

"Do we have an agreement?" Dante asked.

"You know the answer to that," Michael replied.

"I want to hear you say it," Dante demanded. "Your word, after all, is your bond."

"Fine. We have an agreement... until a key shows up, that is or you change the terms."

"I expected no less from you," Dante stated, pressing a button that unlocked the leg restraints. "Come. I'll show you around a bit and we can grab a drink... for old time's sake. No sense being enemies until the occasion arises."

"Before we do," Michael said, "could I trouble you for something else to wear? This robe is a bit drafty. While I change, you might explain to me how you haven't aged. You haven't had access to the same means as I."

Dante laughed. "Let's just say when we do come head-to-head... and we will, I'm going to have to kill you. Rest assured, your blood will go to good use."

Chapter Eighteen

Tara coughed. The meager contents of her stomach emptied onto the stone floor. She gasped, taking in as many shallow breaths of air as she could. For a moment, she wondered how much she had to drink the night before - a pounding head indicating it had been quite a party.

Tea. She chuckled, instantly regretting her laughter. Another round of vomit joined the pile beside her. Her mother's night time tea never had this effect on her.

She glanced around. There wasn't much to look at. She was in some sort of a cave. There was no furniture and no doors. Stone was all she could see. There was no odour, or dampness, indicating in her mind this area must have been manmade to look like a cave rather than actually being one.

"Hello," she stuttered, her throat still burning from stomach acid. Her throat cleared. "Hello." She tried to stand, but between her hands being tied behind her back and her still shaky equilibrium she merely managed to end up on her stomach, feeling like a tied hog.

"Good!" Mrs. Filmore exclaimed. "You are finally awake. We've been keeping some very important people waiting. They aren't the patient sort. To be honest, none of the virtues are their strong suit." She sliced the rope bindings on Tara's wrists.

"Waiting for what?" Tara asked, rolling over and immediately grasping her head. The pounding sensation worsened with movement.

"To meet you, of course," Mrs. Filmore replied.

"What was in that tea?" Tara asked.

"It was a little stronger than usual," Mrs. Filmore stated, grabbing her arm. "Up you come."

"Wait!" Tara exclaimed, pulling away. "Last night... I remember. You said you killed my parents."

"I suppose I did," Mrs. Filmore said, shrugging her shoulders. "That doesn't change anything. I still need to get you ready."

"Doesn't change anything?!" Tara yelled. "You killed my parents... you were friends with them. Why?"

"You are being a tad dramatic, my dear," Mrs. Filmore replied. "None of you were ever my friends."

"But..."

"Oh," Mrs. Filmore interrupted, holding a finger in the air. "They were my husband's friends. I suppose that counts for something. Did you know I was born into this mess? I was given no choices in life.

Protecting the bloodline was all I ever heard - even growing up. A husband was chosen for me. I played my part and married him - all to protect you. One day, the chosen descendant would come - blah, blah, blah. I thought it was all a joke, or at least I'd never see it in my lifetime. Then you came along. It wasn't until recently that any of us realized it was you our ancestors were going on about. You don't really fit the part."

"You didn't love him?" Tara asked. "Your husband?"

"I respected him, but no, I didn't love him," Mrs. Filmore answered. "Then a man came to me. Not just any man, of course - the most beautiful man I had ever met. He swept me off my feet. For the first time, I felt what it was like to be in love. On top of that, he had a way to make me young again. All I had to do was give him what he wanted."

"Me," Tara mumbled.

"Yes. You met him, picking up his order," Mrs. Filmore agreed. "Everything was going as planned until that other group of demons tried to snatch you. Then your mother stuck her nose in. I tried to calm her down some. That's when I learnt you hadn't yet been told about your heritage. I made a few calls and tried to rush the kidnapping, but that horseman got in the way. It was one thing after another."

"Why go back and kill them?"

"It wasn't the plan, of course," Mrs. Filmore said. "Dante was less than pleased with me for not delivering you. Failure does carry consequences. I needed to find you. I thought your parents might be hiding you. Once they figured out I had switched sides, I couldn't let them live. They would have hunted me down. You have to understand, I already had my hands full with Dante's men. That's why I was ready for a fight last night. I honestly thought I was done for. Then to my surprise, you waltzed in and saved the day."

"You killed my parents for a man?!" Tara yelled.

"I killed them for my freedom!" Mrs. Filmore exclaimed. "I don't expect you to understand. I do, however, expect you to do what I say."

"Why should I?" Tara snapped.

Mrs. Filmore placed two fingers in her mouth and delivered a loud soccer-mom whistle. A wrinkled finger pointed to six male guards - eyes bulging in her direction. "I can take you, bathe you and change you... or they can. Believe me, they would have no issue with taking advantage of a woman. There are no instructions to keep you untouched. It's your choice."

Tara glanced between the perverted leers of the guards and Mrs. Filmore. "Fine," she whispered. "I'll do what you want." She bit her bottom lip, holding back a building anger and a rising need for revenge. She'd bide her time, for now. When the opportunity presented itself, she'd be more than willing to take it.

"That's a good girl," Mrs. Filmore said. "There's a pretty dress waiting for you after you clean up. This way."

Tara pushed past the guards, following Mrs. Filmore to an adjoining room through a secret passageway. She glanced back at the wall as it closed.

"Don't worry," Mrs. Filmore stated. "They won't enter unless I call or you take too long. Strip down." She nodded to a pool of water with fresh rose petals floating on top. "You need a bath before dressing."

"What's in it?" Tara asked.

"Nothing that will hurt you," Mrs. Filmore replied. "You're the guest of honour. I'd hurry if I were you. We have a schedule to keep. If the guards don't drag you out on time, Dante will - dressed or not."

Tara had never believed in karma before, but at that moment she prayed it was real and would find Mrs. Filmore guilty of committing atrocities.

Chapter Nineteen

At first, Tara imagined the outfit she'd be wearing as being an all-white flowing gown. The thought of being a sacrifice to a God she had never even heard of before made her change the vision. The next was just as bad - a flowery dress from Mrs. Filmore's closet. She'd already lived through the nightmare of that once before and once was definitely enough for her.

"Don't just stand there staring at it," Mrs. Filmore snapped. "Put it on. It's your size."

The dress she'd actually been given was more stunning than anything she'd ever seen before. Made from a cream colour, highlighted with gold threads and lace, it was befitting of a goddess. Whoever designed it matched the colour to her skin tone with perfection. With an open back design it was hard to tell where the dress ended and she began. As Mrs. Filmore had suggested, it fit perfectly - as if made to order from one of the world's finest designers.

If she wasn't about to be led to certain doom, she might have enjoyed playing dress-up.

"Sit," Mrs. Filmore ordered.

"Ow!" Tara screamed. "That hurt."

"If you would stay still and stop wiggling, it would hurt less," Mrs. Filmore stated, pulling a brush through another tangle. "What good is a gorgeous gown if you have matted frizzy hair? Honestly. Don't you ever brush this mop?"

"I haven't had a brush handy," Tara complained. "It's not like I had time to pack a bag."

After a few pokes and a whole lot of pulling, a gold hair net was attached to the back of her head, holding her hair in place with elegance. Tara gazed into the crude mirror she was handed - hardly recognizing herself. The transformation was incredible.

"There we are," Mrs. Filmore said. "No make-up or fake scents. Dante hates that on women."

"Why do I want to impress Dante?" Tara asked. "I thought you were in love with him. Shouldn't you be impressing him?"

"There will be plenty of time for that when I am young again," Mrs. Filmore cooed. "Until then, I am impressing him by following his orders exactly as he demands. Then when the time is right, he has promised to take me by his side."

"What happened to Michael?" Tara asked.

"The horseman?" Mrs. Filmore replied, chuckling. "He's not a bad catch, either. You might have given up your chance to take a peek, but I definitely didn't. That man could make any woman happy. The equipment he has available is..."

"What did you do?"

"Oh, don't get yourself all in a sweat," Mrs. Filmore said. "I just took a quick look-see. Besides, he isn't the man for you. If he was, he'd be trying to rescue you instead of having a lager with his old friend. He was using you. Mark my words, his only interest is in getting his hands on that key - not your body." She laughed. "You should have taken your chance while you could. Personally, I'm regretting not taking a few pictures. If that horseman is any indication, demigods have a lot more to offer a girl than ordinary men." She fanned herself with one hand. "Now, getting those two both together at the same time," she moaned.

"That's disgusting. You're..."

"Old?" Mrs. Filmore asked. "Only my body is old and that won't be for long. I suppose you are still upset he isn't playing your knight in white armour. One might expect the bad guys not to care what happens to you, but the good guys not caring either - that's just sad."

Tara took in a few short breaths. She bit her bottom lip, her hands shaking. "You're lying."

"Another heartbreak," Mrs. Filmore said. "Poor dear, what will you do? You shouldn't have gotten so involved so quickly. It's a good thing you aren't wearing mascara with those tears." She tossed a handkerchief at Tara. "Dry your eyes. We don't have time for you to be sentimental. Let's go. They are waiting for us."

"What do they want with me?" Tara asked.

"I have no idea," Mrs. Filmore replied. "That information is above my pay grade - so to speak. I do know, when they are done, one of them will be holding the key to the first gate." She laughed. "That is what the horseman came for, isn't it? I already told you, the key was all he was after the whole time. I am sure you fantasized he was here to protect you. That's normal for a girl like you with an overactive imagination. Truth be told, there is no one left who cares enough about you to do that. Your parents were the last ones who did and look what that got them."

Tara felt as if she'd been kicked in the stomach. The urge to vomit returned. She gulped back pooling saliva, trying to avoid further angering the evil woman leading her like a farm animal to slaughter.

She chuckled under her breath. Perhaps her first instinct had been correct. There was a very good chance she was about to become a sacrifice in some sick ritual. She shivered at the thought. A part of her wanted to run. That part was soon lost to a more powerful one - the part of her that would welcome death, realizing how truly alone she was.

Chapter Twenty

With a clash of frosted beer mugs and a round of laughter, the two warriors were as they once had been. It didn't take much for Michael to sink right back into a place he had thought lost long ago. He'd missed his friend and until that moment, he hadn't realized how much. When they were together, it was as if nothing could stop them. Together they could face the world and overcome any obstacle in their paths - a true force to be reckoned with.

Still, the survival instincts that had kept him alive for years took notice of his surroundings. They were in what he could only describe as an officer's lounge. There was ample flowing ale and shots of whiskey on demand. The furniture was wooden and lacked comfort, but was easily replaceable if a fight broke out, which from the looks of a few repaired pieces, happened often. There was only one door leading in or out. He'd already figured out they were inside a mountain or underground.

"Sir," a guard said, interrupting the reunion.

Dante nodded. "Well," he said. "As fun as this has been, we have an appointment to keep. It looks like it's time." He patted Michael on the back. "I wish things were different. I have missed you, old friend." He motioned with one hand to follow the guards into a corridor.

"What is this place?" Michael asked.

"A series of hidden caverns and tunnels," Dante explained. "They were used for hundreds of years, then sealed up as unsafe. It took a bit of work, but we made them usable again. Forgive me if I don't tell you the exact location."

Michael stopped at a ledge overlooking a large room below. The upper level they stood on acted as nothing more than a balcony for viewing.

"You have to be kidding," Michael snickered, pointing to a number of hooded figures being led into the ceremony beneath them. "This looks like a bad budget cult movie."

"What were you hoping for?" Dante asked.

Michael's eyebrows arched and lips pursed together. "I don't know, but something more than this. It's rather cliché, don't you think?"

"Perhaps," Dante replied. "But we do have to follow the ritual as it is written. I'm not leaving anything to chance."

"Did you ever think that someone might be pulling your leg?" Michael commented. "Maybe the scrolls aren't real. That would be a good joke."

Dante laughed. "I assure you the scrolls are real - as is this ceremony. I verified everything myself." He took the lead, heading down spiral steps. "Bees wax candles are used from here on. Everything is all natural." The stairs led to a small room full of black cloaks. "Even the cloaks were spun from virgin wool and handcrafted."

"Your own personal sweatshop, no doubt. Child slave labour, perhaps?" Michael asked. "You're going to make me wear one of those, aren't you?"

"I'm afraid I must insist," Dante replied. "Everyone in attendance must wear a robe. It doesn't matter where they were made or by whom. It is part of the ritual."

"If I refuse?" Michael asked.

"The ceremonial altar and adjoining space has been sanctified. According to procedures, anyone entering without the proper attire may be subjected to sacrifice," Dante explained, pulling the hood over his head. "Your choice."

"Feel silly or feel dead," Michael muttered, shrugging his shoulders. He accepted a robe from his former friend. "I suppose I owe it to the world to at least find out what this ritual is all about. I have to admit, this robe is better than the last one."

Dante laughed. "Come then. The preparations for the arrival of Nakamire's kin are underway."

Michael moved into a position in front of a round pillar located behind the altar. He glanced around the room, surveying the situation. It was inevitable a battle was coming. His only hope for survival was preparation. Unfortunately, the room itself only had three ways out: one the way he came in; and two more on the far side. From the way the place was now filling, it appeared as if there would be hundreds to go through to get to one of those.

On top of attendees, there were also four guards, equipped with spears and swords, stationed on the inside of each door and a dozen more at various stations along the walls. Those were the ones he could see. Potentially, there were more outside.

The altar was prepared with a cream and gold cloth. Gold candlesticks held wax pillars, already lit. A variety of golden, jewel encrusted blades were laid out in a circle, waiting for use. A cloaked figure moved forward and ran each of the blades through candle fire while chanting words meaning purification in no particular order.

From the altar he counted four steps down to a pit, inside of which was the only thing he couldn't see from where he stood. Two men, painted gold, wearing nothing but cream loincloths, came forward with torches. They took positions on either side of the gully, chanting the words *fire of life* over and over in every known language possible. The two torches dropped. The pit exploded into flames, reaching almost to the ceiling.

"And so it begins," Dante said, raising his hands up high. The rest of the congregation copied his words and movements before falling to their knees and bowing down.

"Open the doors and bring forth the one through whom the blood of Nakamire runs!" Dante yelled. "For it is her blood that shall reveal to us the key."

The words *the key* echoed through the masses. Two large doors opened, revealing a procession ready to parade in. The crowd split, forming a clear path to the pit of fire.

A man carrying a gold banner with embossed flames entered. His attire was the same cream and gold as the altar. He stopped at the fire, turning to face the rest of his party. Behind him, several younger men and women followed. Each of them dressed in black, hooded tunics with a red crest of a serpent climbing out of flames - in such a manner as to suggest the slithering creature was being born from the fire. Men formed lines on the left and women on the right, acting more as a form of crowd control than anything else.

Michael tilted his head to one side, wondering why Mrs. Filmore was the next in line - in her normal clothes. That couldn't be proper attire. The thought didn't last long, as he caught the first glimpse of Tara being escorted by guards down the aisle. His mind raced, trying to find anything to compare to the beauty he was witnessing at that moment. There was nothing. He shifted his weight between legs, glad the robe was covering the proof of his growing attraction. He held his breath, trying to offset the effects of panic setting in. He realized for the first time he had no idea exactly what they planned to do to her. He also knew he wouldn't be able to stand by and watch.

"The fire of the serpent be tamed with this offering of a woman's flesh!" Dante yelled.

Michael poised to spring, but stumbled back into his place as he watched Mrs. Filmore's body engulf in flames. One scream was all she voiced before her end. Two guards grabbed Tara as her knees buckled, dragging her across a bridge that formed through the fire. They tossed her on the ground at Dante's feet.

Michael's heart ached as he watched; tears stream down Tara's face. He could feel the fear racing through her body causing her to shake. The odds of either of them escaping were slim to none. If he was going to die, it was going to be trying to save the woman he loved. Hopes of hanging on until the key was exposed before acting were fading fast.

Michael's gaze met hers. She looked away quickly. It had been long enough for him to see pain in her eyes - pain that he had caused. She believed he had betrayed her and, in a way, he had. He had been willing to sacrifice her safety in hopes of finding the key.

"Bring forth the cage!" Dante ordered.

A trap door in the ceiling opened, allowing a metal cage to be lowered. The structure was shaped like a sarcophagus, but built with bars rather than made of stone. A chain attached to the top rattled as it came closer to them. The tips of sharp blades were visible on the inside. From the looks of them, it didn't look like a little blood was all they planned to use. Michael took two steps forward.

Dante motioned for him to remain where he stood. "We aren't going to kill her- relax."

"That doesn't look like you aren't going to harm her," Michael argued, watching the cage swing slightly.

Dante laughed. "I didn't say it wasn't going to hurt. Still, we have no intentions of killing her. We need her for three more ceremonies, after all. Keeping her alive is a priority. Her condition, however, is of no concern. She doesn't need to look the part of a beautiful sacrifice after tonight and I assure you after those blades cut in, she won't."

Michael gasped. "You didn't mention that before, old friend. I'm afraid this is where I get off this ride." Swords appeared in both hands. He aimed the first strike at Dante's head, barely missing. The next attack, metal hit metal - his mentor now armed. Sparks flew wildly as swords met in a series of blows. Neither party faltered.

Tara screamed. Her pleas for help drew Michael's attention. He barely avoided Dante's latest strike. He jumped on to the altar, looking for a better position to watch Tara from while in combat. The guards tossed her into the cage like a rag doll, shutting the door and motioning that it was secured.

Dante matched his move. "Pull it up!" he commanded. "It's over. You can't save her now."

Michael watched the cage begin to rise, Tara locked inside. There was only one chance. With a running start, he sprung forward, using a guard's head as a step. He barely managed to grip the bottom of the contraption before it raised beyond reach. They swung wildly - a result of his added weight. Using his upper body strength, he pulled himself up.

"Hey," he said.

"Hey," Tara echoed, her voice wavering. "What are you doing?"

"Saving you, of course," Michael answered. He grasped the cage door and pulled. Nothing happened. He sighed. "This is going to take some pressure. I need you to hang on tight." He strained every muscle tugging on the locked door. A few choice swear words escaped under his breath. Of course, it had to be made of the experimental metal. It would have been easier if they were on solid ground; every push and pull made the cage swing recklessly.

"Give up!" Dante yelled. "From that position, it isn't possible even for you to open that cage." He turned to the congregation watching. "Bring it back down."

"We can't," a guard answered. "It has to lodge at the top before it can be released again. That is the way the scrolls described."

Michael pulled again, this time applying all his strength to the lock. It snapped. After that, he made short work of the hinges. The door swung off, falling to the ground. Tara screamed, almost slipping from inside as the cage swung to the side.

"Hang on," Michael said. "Don't let go of the bar." He ducked out of the way of a barrage of several spears lobbed from the guards below. It was lucky Dante hadn't trained them in the finer art of spear combat. The thought lingered as odd for a split-second. Dante was a master with spears. If he wanted the demons to truly have a fighting chance, he should have trained the guards personally. The sloppy work he was witnessing was only a bit better than one would see in a low budget movie.

"Get up there. Cut them off if they make it to the top!" Dante ordered. "Quickly."

The room cleared with the exception of a handful of guards. Another mistake. The cage jolted to a stop before reversing directions. Michael swung his body inside the cage, a blade piercing his side. Blood trickled out, soaking his shirt. With one arm around Tara's waist and the other holding onto a bar, he surveyed his choices. Removing his cloak, he dropped it on the guards below, knocking several over in confusion.

"Get ready," he whispered. "Hang on to my back. I'm going to jump. We need to clear the guards. Once we do, head for the far doors."

Tara nodded. He could feel her shakiness begin to dissipate in his arms. She had faith in him and he wasn't going to let her down. He had already done enough of that for one day. He stood at the opening, forcing the cage to sway back and forth like a midway ride.

"On three," he said. "One; two; three." At the top of the next swing he jumped, landing on the far side of the room. Tara slid off his back.

Michael seized the opportunity and spun around to meet a half a dozen guards. It took no more than four strikes to eliminate them all. He glanced briefly at Dante still at the altar. His old friend smiled and bowed before exiting out the back way. There was no time to interpret the move; changing directions, he ran out the door, Tara in tow.

Chapter Twenty-One

The corridors all looked the same. The only thing Michael knew for sure was they needed to head up. Given a choice to go straight or take stairs, he chose the stairs.

He could hear Tara's breathing become erratic. There was no possible way her legs would be able to keep up the pace he had set and needed to keep. He stopped and threw her over his shoulder without protest.

The upstairs hallway led them into a circular room with multiple exits. A group of three guards blocked their movements. Without setting Tara down, he summoned a one-handed sword and entered combat. The first two enemies fell with ease. The third, he pinned to the stone wall.

"Which way?!" Michael yelled. He shook the guard by the shoulder. "Which way or I gut you on the spot!"

The guard didn't speak - he didn't need to. His eyes revealed the answer they needed with a simple glance towards one of the doors. Michael released him - the blade slicing through his midsection. The guard's body fell into a slumped pile on the ground, succumbing to his wound.

"I thought you weren't going to kill him!" Tara shrieked, still upside down, her face flushed red.

"I never said I wouldn't," Michael answered. "If I left him, he would have called a hundred more. We are in survival mode. That means we can't afford to leave any loose ends. If I find one, I'll make sure it gets tied up neatly in any manner I can."

"But... you could handle them if they came. Right?" Tara asked. "I mean... you are immortal."

"There are always ways in which we can die," Michael explained. "While I am stronger than most, I am unfortunately not invincible."

"So you can die..."

"Yes," Michael replied.

"You're telling me this now? Why are you risking your life for me?" Tara screamed, slapping him on the butt.

Michael laughed. "Because I choose to," he answered. "I'll make you a deal. If we make it out of this alive, you can repay me with a date. Slap me on the butt again and I might have to find a place to claim you as my mate right now."

Tara gasped, pulling her hands to her chest, not sure if her prince charming was joking or not. She wasn't about to take any chances. A bed of rock would be rather uncomfortable for a claiming.

Michael pulled the door open to a set of stairs which led to a much different scene. He recognized the layout - sewer tunnels. He chuckled to himself. It was no wonder no one had found that demon hideout before. Who would think to look for a place under a city's sewer system? It was ingenious and stinky. He breathed through his mouth, trying to move as quickly as possible to a higher level.

Michael could see exactly what he was looking for. Up ahead, there was an opening to a small room. If the schematics of this city were similar to all the others he had seen, it contained little other than a ladder leading to a manhole exit in a street. He raced inside with little thought other than reaching fresh air.

"Going somewhere?" a demon cackled.

Michael swiveled around, coming face-to-face with a winged woman, her face wrinkled and distorted. He set Tara down beside him. "You must be one of Dante's wives. He mentioned the wings," he commented, pointing to the creature's black feathers. "I'm afraid he didn't mention your name, though."

The demon laughed. "Don't worry. I always tell my name to those I am about to feed on. I'm Creta. Dante didn't tell me a thing about you - other than he wants you dead and the woman returned." She smiled, revealing razor-sharp, black teeth.

"And here I was thinking you wanted to show me the way out," Michael snickered. "You still could. If you did, I wouldn't have to slice those wings from your back and mail them to your husband."

Creta shrieked, a deafening noise he'd never heard before. This demon was a new level of disgusting. He winced, remembering the story his old friend had told him about being forced to mate with it. Dante's anger was a little more understandable now he was face-to-face with the horror he had been forced to live with.

The demon lunged forward, claws growing out of her fingers. She swiped at him in passing, leaving a gash in his side - the one that wasn't already bleeding. Michael retaliated - two swords appearing, one in each hand. He rushed forward swinging. Steel hit flesh and bone. Creta cried out in pain.

Michael had done what he said he would. Two black feather wings lay at his feet. He kicked them aside, narrowly dodging a new attack. The demon woman fueled by rage turned and slashed at his face. He'd been too preoccupied to see a second demon enter the fight. A novice battle mistake that should have cost him his life.

"Look out!" Tara screamed, pushing Michael out of danger. She crouched down on the ground, awaiting punishment for her bravery. Nothing happened. She inhaled deeply, her nostrils recognizing the floral scents she loved from her childhood. The same scents of the bouquets that had sat on her nightstand - the ones that kept demons at bay.

"What were you thinking?" Michael yelled, helping Tara to her feet. "You must really want that date. Nice job, by the way." He winked. "When did you learn to make a flower shield? I've never seen anything like it before. You were holding out on me."

"I don't know what you mean," Tara stuttered. "What happened?"

"You don't know?" Michael asked, scratching his neck. "You pushed me out of the way and made a flower barrier between us and the demons. They couldn't handle it and ran off."

"I did that?"

"Yeah," Michael said. "It's not a bad trick to have in your arsenal. Let's get out of here. I have a date to plan."

Tara grabbed the ladder and began to climb. "It better be a good one, too. If what you say is true, I did just save your life."

Michael laughed. "I suppose you did. I think I'm still two up on you, though."

Chapter Twenty-Two

"You two look and smell like death warmed up," Gabby said, waving a hand in front of her nose. "What on earth have you been doing? Playing in raw sewage?"

"Good to see you too, sis," Michael replied.

"Don't even think about touching any furniture until you've both had showers and are wearing clean clothes," Gabby ordered, shooing them away.

Tara gladly accepted the suggestion and headed to the room she'd be given earlier.

"Dante is alive," Michael blurted out.

"What?" Gabby shrieked. "That's not possible. We all saw him fall. You searched for the body."

"A couple demon spawn grabbed him," Michael explained. "They nursed him back to health in exchange for his seed."

"His seed? You mean there is a demigod-demon hybrid out there somewhere?" Gabby shook her head. "Even so," she argued, "his age..."

"He's found a way to counter the effects of aging," Michael interrupted. "I don't exactly know how, but it involves drinking blood and some other rituals. He didn't go into details."

"Where is he?" Gabby asked.

"He's leading the demons in the hunt for the keys," Michael replied. "Some of it just doesn't make sense to me."

"Some of it?" Gabby shrieked. "None of what you said makes sense to me. He actually changed sides? Did he fight you?"

"That's what's bothering me," Michael answered. "He was always stronger than I was. Even with all the training I've had since, he should have easily given me a run for my money. Our fight was more a spar than a battle. Neither one of us broke a sweat."

"You're saying he didn't try?"

"I'm saying he made it look good," Michael explained. "I'm not sure what he is doing. He sent one of his demon women after me instead of coming himself. He should have known I could best her on my worst day. There were so many little mistakes, the Dante I knew never would have made. There is more going on than meets the eye."

"Do you think he's playing double agent?" Gabby asked.

"I'm not sure he's on our side, either," Michael said, staring into the distance. "It could very well be he is playing his own tune in all this - one without loyalties."

"Or he could have been testing you to see how much strength you've picked up over the past centuries," Gabby suggested. "Lose the battle today to win the war tomorrow is a strong strategy."

"That's true," Michael admitted. "I guess only time will tell. There's more."

"Why do I feel like I should be sitting down?" Gabby asked, pulling out a chair.

"Dante has found a scroll outlining how to find one of the keys," Michael stated. "It involves using the blood of a descendant. That's why they wanted Tara."

"If they need Tara, she should stay here," Gabby suggested. "Then they won't be able to perform the ceremony."

"I agree - she is staying," Michael replied, rubbing his neck. "Dante did, however, mention there were other scrolls and other descendants. That gives us all something else to worry about. Apparently, any one of the descendants can be used in all the rituals. At least that's what Dante is anticipating."

"Does he have them?"

"No," Michael said, exhaling loudly. "He was waiting to see if the first ritual worked before going after the others."

"That at least gives us a bit of time," Gabrielle replied, taking notes in a journal. "More has happened in the past week than in centuries of living. I think we may be finding out what Nakamire's master plan was."

"Something else happened," Michael commented. "Tara made a flower shield appear in the middle of a battle. She very well might have saved me from injury."

"Are you sure?" Gabby asked. "I've never heard of anyone being able to materialize flowers to use as a defence. Which types?"

"The same as grow in the gardens," Michael replied.

"I'll do some research," Gabby offered. "I have a few theories I'd like to check out."

"Great. I'm going to take that shower." He nodded towards the door. "Keep Tara company for me while I'm gone."

"That feels better," Tara said, entering the room.

Michael stopped in passing to give her a once-over. He winked. "That looks great on you."

Tara smiled. "Thanks - to you, too, Gabby for lending me clothes. I was a little concerned about what I was going to wear."

"It's no problem," Gabby answered. "That dress looks much better on you than it ever did on me. Of course, now you are going to be staying here, we'll have to make a shopping trip so you have your own things."

"Staying here?" Tara asked. "I hadn't realized I would be staying. Are you sure?"

Gabby laughed. "Don't expect Michael to ask. He's more an assumption kind of guy. I think you are stuck with him."

Tara bit the corner of her bottom lip. "I'm not sure I understand everything that's going on," she admitted. "I do know that I am not like you."

"You're worried about aging, aren't you?" Gabby asked. "You don't need to be. This house is magic. It's a little pocket of space that imitates the place the Gods came from. Anyone who has the blood of a God running through their veins, who comes here in regular intervals, will not age. That includes you. If this is your home, you'll be fine."

"So I'll stay this age forever?" Tara asked, eyebrows arched.

"We estimate aging to stop at about twenty-five of this world's years," Gabby answered. "That doesn't mean you can't die. We are all susceptible to death. The world is what we make of it. If it perishes, we all do. This is, for all intents and purposes, our reward for keeping the planet safe."

Tara shook her head. "I don't know what I can do to help. A few days ago, I didn't even know demons and Gods were real."

"That," Gabby replied, "is something we need to figure out. Michael mentioned you developed an interesting ability. I've never heard of a flower shield before. I have some ideas on the subject, but I'll need to do a bit more investigating before I come up with anything solid. I'd like you to practice calling various flowers while I do research."

"I don't know how," Tara admitted. "They appeared. I don't remember doing anything. I don't even remember them. My eyes were closed the whole time."

"Try thinking back to the moment before," Gabby suggested. "Create the same emotions you were feeling."

"Complete and utter fear?" Tara muttered. "I'm not sure I can create that." She clenched her eyes tight with furrowed brow. Her face turned a light shade of pink.

"You have to breathe!" Gabby exclaimed. "Maybe don't try so hard. It's something you can work with over time. No one expects you to figure it out this minute. You have a long life ahead."

"But if I could," Tara said, "it would help defeat them - the demons? That's what you are hoping."

"I never speculate," Gabby explained. "I only give information I can back up with facts. That's a rule I made for myself. I will, however, say I believe you are here for a purpose. If I am right, perhaps more than one." She nodded towards Michael standing in the doorway. "Looks like someone is waiting for you. I'll be reading if you need me. I doubt you will, though. Have fun."

"You ready for that date?" Michael asked, a mischievous smile creeping over his lips.

Chapter Twenty-Three

The wind whistled past Tara's ears, producing a sharp bite that put colour in her cheeks. She'd always wanted to try horseback riding, but her parents, for one reason or another, never took her. Now, with Michael's arms wrapped around her waist, she felt like this was where she was always meant to be.

"I told you we had the horses," Michael teased. "Do you like him? He seems to have taken to you."

"Yes," Tara replied. What wasn't to like? Michael's horse was a pure black stallion named Damion - a name which, when she first heard it, had made her choke. Perhaps she'd watched a few too many horror films, but that word she always associated with evil and something this creature was far from.

Michael motioned and Damion changed directions. The sun was setting, leaving a chill in the air. Tara sighed under her breath. The afternoon had flown by far too fast. Every moment she spent there seemed to make it easier to believe she had found her true home.

She swallowed back the guilt of her parents' death. They had raised her and looked out for her. A sudden thought overpowered her. One of them had to be a blood relation to Nakamire as well.

"Are you with me?" Michael asked, holding his hand up to help her dismount.

She'd been so consumed by her own thoughts she hadn't even noticed they'd already arrived back at the stables. "Sorry," she muttered, taking his hand.

"Daydreaming?" Michael asked, holding out a few cubes of sugar as a reward for his steed's good behaviour.

"Something like that," she mumbled. "I was thinking." Her hand gently stroked the stallion's nose.

"Must be pretty deep thoughts," Michael chuckled, motioning towards the exit.

"They are," she replied, following him through the gardens.

Michael stopped and pulled her close. "Penny for your thoughts," he said. He leaned in, their lips almost touching.

"I hope I'm not interrupting," Gabby announced.

"You are," Michael groaned, releasing his grip.

"Sorry," Gabby said, offering a fake smile as compensation and shrugging her shoulders. "I wanted to talk to you before I left."

"Where are you going?" Michael asked, arching his brows. "You hate leaving the house."

"I need to do some research that I can't do here," Gabby explained. "I'll be gone for several weeks, so you two will have to take care of the place. You'll be the only ones here, so no one else can interrupt whatever it is I interrupted." She giggled.

"Can I ask a question?" Tara stuttered, raising her hand. She didn't wait for an answer. "If I am a direct descendant of Nakamire, wouldn't that make one of my parents his blood relative as well?"

"Yes," Gabby said.

"That's a good point," Michael agreed. "Why didn't they use your mother or father in the ritual?"

"What do you mean?" Gabby asked.

"The demons only went after Tara," Michael stated. "Her parents were killed. If they only needed the blood of Nakamire's relative, they could have used one of them."

"There must be something special about Tara," Gabby replied.

"Mrs. Filmore said something before she died," Tara said, realizing for the first time karma had found its mark. "She said that they were waiting for the right ancestor to show up and she hadn't expected this to happen in her lifetime."

"That actually makes a bit of sense. If I am right, there are three others we still need to find. Leave finding the answers to me. You two take a bit of a vacation." Gabby over exaggerated a wink.

"Take a cell phone," Michael called to her back. "Let Uri and Ralph know you are out there."

Gabby waved her hand over her head. "Have fun."

"So," Michael said, pulling Tara back. "Where were we?"

"You were about to tell me what we are doing for the rest of this date," Tara joked.

Michael leaned in and lightly brushed the tip of her nose with his lips. "I thought I'd make you dinner, then we could watch a movie. I was hoping you might explain to me all about roleplaying gatekeeper and keymaster."

Tara laughed. "You would have to remember that," she joked. Using her tip toes, she kissed his cheek.

"Not good enough," he whispered, taking advantage of the opportunity. Their lips met, desperately trying to satisfy a hunger that had been growing inside both of them.

A moan escaped her throat. She felt complete. This was the part of her life that had been missing. There would be no more trying to fit in - no more failures. She was home.

"No more worrying," Michael whispered, brushing her hair behind one of her ears. "The ball is in Gabby's court now. We'll let her run with it. At least for the moment."

Tara nodded. That sounded perfect to her.

Author's Message

I hope you enjoyed reading Michael and Tara's story as much as I did writing it. Be sure to watch social media or my website for more Four Horsemen Novels coming soon.

Thank you for reading! If you enjoyed this story, please browse through some on my other titles currently available.

The Portal Prophecies

These great titles in C.A. King's The Portal Prophecies series are available now at most online book retailers:

A Keeper's Destiny

A Halloween's Curse

Frost Bitten

Sleeping Sands

Deadly Perceptions

Finding Balance

The prophecies are the key to their survival. Can they solve them in time?

Tomoiya's Story

A Vampire Tale. She had a secret, but she wasn't the only one with something to hide.

Escape to Darkness

Collecting Tears

When Leaves Fall: A different Point of View Story

Ralph wakes up to what others only experience in a nightmare. Chained to a shed, he has no idea where he is, or who his captor is. His memories are blurred at best. As the days press on, he finds himself experiencing a roller coaster of feelings. Hunger, thirst and pain become his only companions. Flashbacks of a happier time are all he has to keep him going. As his situation deteriorates, he finds himself doubting the very things he wants most - a family.

When Leaves Fall is a dramatic thriller with a twist. Keep the tissue box close for the ending.

Peach Coloured Daisies: A Cursed by the Gods Story

He couldn't die. An ancient curse meant she always did. This time, that was going to change - one way or another.

When Daisy's grandmother, her last living relative, passes away, she doesn't know where to turn. Things go from bad to worse when a local psychic tells her about a curse. Alone and confused, she ends up in front of her college professor's office, ready to cry her heart out in his arms.

Matt Demi might be the son of a God, but he's living the life of a cursed man. He's had to watch the woman he loves die on her twenty-first birthday countless times. Nothing he does seems to be able to affect the outcome. When she shows up at his office scared out of her wits by a psychic's prediction, he vows this time will be different.

With only three days, Matt will need to embrace a side of him he swore off long ago to save her, but will he lose himself in the process?

Other titles coming soon from C.A. King

Shattering the Effect of Time

Join the Shinning brother, Jessie, Dezi and Pete as they set out on quest for a way to save their younger sister. No magic known to them or their friends can reverse the grip of time. There are a few legends that mention ancient items that may hold the key to do exactly that. This brand new series will take you on a search for the fountain of youth and mermaids; a quest for the holy grail; a trip to visit Daryl the mountain guru in the hunt for the Cinamani Stone; searching for ambrosia from the gods; and other adventures.

Surviving the Sins

The prophecies are being rewritten. This time someone is using the seven deadly sins: Lust; Gluttony; Greed; Sloth; Wrath; Envy; and Pride, to unlock an ancient evil. The book falls into Jade's hands to answer destiny's call. Can she survive the sins?